PENGUIN  CL

A TALE OF FOUR DERVISHES

MIR AMMAN was born in Delhi into a family of distinguished retainers at the Mughal Court, some time in the second half of the eighteenth century. Forced to leave the city of his ancestors at the close of the century owing to the declining fortunes of the Mughal Empire, he found employment as a munshi at the British East India Company's Fort William College in Calcutta. It was here that he translated *Bāgh-o-Bahār* (in 1803) and Husain Wāiz Kāshifī's celebrated book on good manners, *Akhalāq-e-Muhsinī*, which was published much later under the title *Ganj-e-Khoobī* (*Treasure House of Virtue*).

MOHAMMED ZAKIR was born in 1932 in Delhi and educated at St Stephen's College, Delhi University, where he took post-graduate degrees in economics and Urdu literature. His main interests have been translation, literary criticism and Urdu linguistics. Among his published works are *Distracting Words*, translations from Ghalib's Urdu and Persian poetry; *The Quintessence of Self-Culture*, a translation of K. G. Saiyidain's writings; *Lessons in Urdu Script*, which has seen several reprints, and some anthologies of Urdu prose and poetry. Presently he is working on a book for English readers on N. M. Rashed, a major Urdu poet. Mohammed Zakir lives in Delhi where he has been teaching Urdu language and literature at the Jamia Millia Islamia for over three decades.

MIR AMMAN

A Tale of Four Dervishes

Translated from the Urdu with an Introduction by
MOHAMMED ZAKIR

PENGUIN BOOKS

This translation is humbly dedicated to my parents
who do not need to read it

PENGUIN BOOKS

Published by the Penguin Group
Penguin Books Ltd, 80 Strand, London WC2R 0RL, England
Penguin Group (USA) Inc., 375 Hudson Street, New York, New York 10014, USA
Penguin Group (Canada), 90 Eglinton Avenue East, Suite 700, Toronto, Ontario, Canada M4P 2Y3
(a division of Pearson Penguin Canada Inc.)
Penguin Ireland, 25 St Stephen's Green, Dublin 2, Ireland (a division of Penguin Books Ltd)
Penguin Group (Australia), 250 Camberwell Road, Camberwell,
Victoria 3124, Australia (a division of Pearson Australia Group Pty Ltd)
Penguin Books India Pvt Ltd, 11 Community Centre,
Panchsheel Park, New Delhi – 110 017, India
Penguin Group (NZ), cnr Airborne and Rosedale Roads, Albany,
Auckland 1310, New Zealand (a division of Pearson New Zealand Ltd)
Penguin Books (South Africa) (Pty) Ltd, 24 Sturdee Avenue,
Rosebank, Johannesburg 2196, South Africa

Penguin Books Ltd, Registered Offices: 80 Strand, London WC2R 0RL, England

www.penguin.com

First published by Penguin India Books 1994
Published in Penguin Classics 2006

008

Copyright © Mohammed Zakir, 1994
All rights reserved

The moral right of the author has been asserted

Printed and bound in Great Britain by Clays Ltd, Elcograf S.p.A.

ISBN-13: 978–0–140–45518–2
ISBN-10: 0–140–45518–3

www.greenpenguin.co.uk

Contents

Introduction

A Tale of Four Dervishes is a translation of Mir Amman's *Bāgh-o-Bahār*, literally 'Garden and Spring'. Itself an Urdu translation cum compilation of earlier Persian and Urdu versions of *Qissa-e-Chahār Darvesh*, which Mir Amman ascribes to Amir Khusrau (d. AD 1325), it has seen several translations and transcriptions in many Indian and European languages. Recent research leads us to believe that the *Qissa* was compiled several years after Khusrau and that its Turkish, Persian and Urdu versions already existed before Mir Amman took it up. Be that as it may, Mir Amman's work remains significant in that it appeared at a time when very little prose literature existed in Urdu for, like many other modern Indo-Aryan languages, Urdu was seldom employed for serious writing. This was done in Persian, the language of the court and administration of Mughal India.

Most of the known prose literature in Urdu, as later traced down from the fourteenth century onwards in the Deccan or in northern India, consisted of tracts, treatises, pamphlets and translations invariably religious in character. The fictional part of it was generally marked by the tendency to use involved sentences and rhyming words. Use of simple, direct prose in fiction, except in a few works which have been unearthed by later researchers, was generally the work of the writers of the Fort William College, Calcutta, established in AD 1800 to acquaint the officers of the English East India Company with the customs and traditions of the people of India. In fact, Mir

Amman must have taken great pains to work out the simplicity and directness of his work and show off in full measure the richness of the Urdu language which was a significant manifestation of the Indo-Muslim culture which originated and flourished after the advent and spread of Islam in India. At times one cannot but feel that there is a fusion here of the Indian and the Islamic Middle Ages, both in methodology and literary ideals.

Early prose in Urdu, as in many other languages, has been more akin to the literature of oral transmission. As such, it needs little introduction. It is the creation of imagination bordering on fancy and is essentially romantic in nature. In Urdu, this genre, known as *dāstān*, has been distinguished more by polished literary presentation than by lofty aims and ideals. It does not pretend to serve any moral purpose, though it has a moral framework and may give us guidelines of good conduct, good government, or virtuous living. In the accounts of the fanciful acts of chivalry and romance, individual responsibility may also have its play in the form of proselytizing zeal.

Structurally akin to the *Arabian Nights*, *Bāgh-o-Bahār* comprises five stories interspersed with several other sub-stories of uneven length and interest, loosely bound together and all with traditionally romantic themes. The four dervishes (and others) who relate their experiences are princes or rich merchants who have renounced the world on account of their unsuccessful love lives. They are guided by a supernatural force to a city where, with the intercession of a king (himself a frustrated man pining for the birth of a son to succeed him) and the help of the king of the djinn, they are reunited with their loves. Typically medieval, the stories describe a magnificent world of romance and affluence—of fairies and the djinn, moonlight and oriental gardens, feasts and ceremonies, and, of course, adventures and mishaps. It is a world where anything might and does happen as man is tossed about by fate. The basic premise, though, is that providence always takes care of us all and that in the end good always triumphs over evil.

As in the *Arabian Nights*, there is no rationality in this work in so far as the treatment of time and space is concerned, yet there is comparatively little that is supernatural in it. Also unlike the *Arabian Nights*, it is not marked by elaborate wooing scenes and erotica or by the frailty and treachery of the fair sex. Though some of the female characters may appear vengeful at times, on the whole they show remarkable courage, faithfulness, integrity and ingenuity. *Bāgh-o-Bahār* thus portrays the more impressive features of Indian womanhood.

Through the genius of the Urdu language, *Bāgh-o-Bahār* affords us a glimpse of the typical Indo-Muslim culture that was prevalent among the cultured classes of India at the time. The stories may be set in Basra, Baghdad, Azerbaijan, Sarandeep, Damascus or Constantinople but the atmosphere is typically that of a Mughal city of India. The weather, the courtly manners, the female guards and personal attendants, the dress, the variety of dishes, festivals and ceremonies, the fireworks, the superstitions and traditions as brought out by the proverbs and apt idioms, are all Indian and bring before us a passing panorama of the Indian elite of the middle ages.

Its interesting tales, its simple and elegant prose as a precursor to the works of the writers of the Delhi College and the Aligarh Movement, its plain yet distinguished style couched in the purity of the idiom, and its portrayal of Indian manners and customs have contributed to make *Bāgh-o-Bahār* a monumental classic of Urdu literature. These qualities have kept it 'green as ever'—still a worthy index of the faiths and beliefs, customs and ceremonies of the people of India.

Very little, in fact no more than what he has written about himself in the preface of the present work, is known about Mir Amman. He hailed from Delhi and after experiencing many vicissitudes in life he finally found employment as a *munshi* at the Fort William College, Calcutta where he translated *Bāgh-o-Bahār*. While there, he also translated Husain Wāiz Kāshifī's celebrated book on good manners, *Akhlāq-e-Muhsinī*, which was published much later under the title *Ganj-e-Khoobī* (*Treasure-house of Virtue*). Recently a critical edition of this work has been published. But it is on *Bāgh-o-Bahār* alone that Mir

Amman's fame rests, and rightly so. Its literary quality and value have never been ignored, nor has it ever ceased being popular as a piece of entertaining literature.

Translation, I believe, is a noble activity as it brings different cultures closer to each other and thus provides for the enrichment of human civilization. It is in this spirit that the present work was undertaken.

With a sense of indebtedness I have availed of the earlier literal translations of the work by Lewis Ferdinand Smith and Duncan Forces, done more than a hundred years ago. My endeavour has been to find the equivalent English idiom without sacrificing the cultural content of Urdu.

I am grateful to those who took the trouble to read the manuscript and offer their comments. Particular thanks are due to Mr L. G. Deo and Mr Muhammad Anas. I am deeply indebted to Mr Zamir Ansari but for whose timely help this translation might not have been published.

March 1987   *Mohammed Zakir*
October 1989

Note. In order to facilitate the printing, footnotes and the diacritical marks have been reduced as much as possible. A glossary has been provided of necessary proper names and words of Indian origin.

PETITION OF MIR AMMAN OF DELHI
TO THE AUTHORITIES OF THE COLLEGE

May God preserve the Exalted Managers and Patrons of noble men. On hearing the proclamation[*], this humble being who has fallen away from his home has composed with great labour and pain, the *Bāgh-o-Bahār* in the *Urdū-e-Mu'allā* language[**] from the *Qissa-e-Chahār Darvesh*. By the grace of God, this 'garden' has been revived by your gracious presence. I hope I may also enjoy its fruits so that the budding desire of my heart also blossoms forth like a rose. About the *Shahnama*, Firdausi[+] says:

> *For thirty years I worked on it and took pains,*
> *And thus I revived Persia by my Persian verse.*

Like him, of my present work I may say:

> *I have polished the Urdu language*
> *And made Bengal a Hindustan[++]*

Gentlemen, you are to judge for yourselves. May the star of your prosperity shine forever!

---

[*] Of Marquess Wellesley, the Governor General of Fort William in Bengal, for promotion of literature in Indian languages among the British personnel.

[**] lit. Language of the Exalted Camp.

[+] Firdausi, Abu'l Qasim (d. AD 1020), the poet of the *Shahnama* (*Book of Kings*) one of the world's greatest epic poems, which stirred the annals of ancient Persia.

[++] Here the author claims that through this work he has introduced the elegance of the Urdu language in Bengal, the chief city of which, Calcutta, was the centre of the East India Company.

Prologue

Glory be to God! What an excellent workman He is! With just a handful of dust, He has created so many diverse faces and figures. Although of two colours, one white and one black, and though He has given to each a nose, ears, hands and feet, even then all of them have distinct features and colours. One is so sharply distinguished from the other in countenance and person that you may easily tell one from the other in the multitude. The sky is a bubble in the Sea of His Unity. And the earth, too, a fragile ball of air; but how so wonderful, the sea beats itself against it yet can cause it no harm. In praise of One who has such power and authority over all, man verily becomes dumb. What words can he find? Silence is better when all eloquence should fail:

> How can I have the power
> To write in praise of One
> Whose work expands from Heaven to the Earth?
> When even the Prophet said,
> 'I could not comprehend Him',
> One will be a great fool
> To make such a claim.
> Day and night the sun and the moon wander
> Through their course to see His works
> But each comes to have
> Only the looks of wonder.
> One whose equal has never been

Nor will there be,
To such an Unique One
To be God suits in every way.
He is the Creator and Nourisher of all.
He has always been graceful and kind to me.

And blessings be on His friend, for whose sake He created the
Earth and Heaven and elevated him to Prophethood:

The pure body of Mustafa
A light emanating from God,
And as is well-known
It cast no shadow.
Where have I the power to utter a word in his praise?
But it is obligatory with poets all.
And blessings be on his progeny, the Twelve Imams!
After the praise of God and the Prophet
Now I mention what I presently propose to do.
May God, for the sake of the progeny of His Prophet
Make what I say acceptable to all.

I undertook this work in AH 1215/AD 1801, corresponding to
1207 Fasli when Lord Mornington, Marquess Wellesley, the
Noble of Nobles, took office as the Governor General and
learning came to be very much in vogue. (One actually finds
oneself at one's wit's end in his praise. He has all the qualities
required of great men. It was the good fortune of this country
that such an ingenious administrator came here. By his charity
and beneficence the majority of people lead a happy life; the
poor pray for his life and prosperity. No one dares tease or
wrong another; the tiger and the goat drink at the same fountain,
as though.) The noble high officials became interested in learning
the Urdu language to be able to converse with Indians and
carry out the administration of the country more effectively.
As such, many books were compiled the same year at his
instance.

A few words about the learned and those who speak the
language of Hindustan. This tale was originally narrated by

Amir Khusrau of Delhi. It so happened that his spiritual guide, Nizamuddin Aulia, the bestower of gold, whose saintly residence was near Lal Bangla, beyond the Matia Darwaza outside the Lal Darwaza, about three miles away from the Fort, was once taken ill. Amir Khusrau was by his bedside. He related this tale to entertain him. By the grace of God, Nizamuddin Aulia was cured of his illness in a few days. The day he took his bath of health, he gave the benediction: 'Whoever hears this tale, will, by the grace of God, remain in health.' Since then it has been quite popular and has had many versions in Persian.

Mr John Gilchrist, the noble and beneficent and a great patron of the noble ones (may he ever remain exalted as long as the Jamuna and the Ganga flow), kindly urged me to render this tale into pure Hindustani which the Urdu people, the Hindus and the Muslims, men and women, young and old, and high and low use in common parlance. As desired by him, I have written it in the conversational style.

First, this humble being prone to sin, Mir Amman of Delhi, begs to say a few words about himself. My ancestors, from generation to generation, served the emperors from the time of Humayun. The emperors exalted them by giving *jagirs* (estates), titles and rewards in plenty. We were called genial retainers, as recorded in the royal archives.

When the great family of rulers (on which rested the prosperity of all others) met such a calamity, which is too well-known to require mention, Suraj Mal Jat confiscated our *jagir* and Ahmad Shah Durrani destroyed our homesteads. Thus I left Delhi (which was my birthplace and where my navel-string is buried). When such a ship (which was steered by the king) was wrecked, I was tossed about on the sea of helplessness and misfortune. A drowning man clutches at a straw, so for a few years I stayed in Azimabad, to have some breathing space. There I saw both good days and bad but ultimately had to leave as I could not have a favourable time there any more. Leaving my family behind I embarked a boat and came to Calcutta, the city of cities, to earn my destined bread. For a

short time I remained unemployed, till one day Nawab Dilavar
Jung sent for me and appointed me tutor to his younger brother,
Mir Muhammad Kazim Khan. I carried on for about two years
and then, realizing that it would not be possible for me to
continue any longer, I managed to get introduced to Mr John
Gilchrist (may he ever remain exalted) through Munshi Mir
Bahadur Ali. It is my good fortune that I found the patronage
of such a benevolent person. So I hope for better days ahead;
otherwise even this I take as a blessing for me. I have bread
to eat. I sleep well. I support the ten members of my family
and they pray for my patron. May God grant their prayers.

A few words about the Urdu language. I have it from my
ancestors that Delhi, according to the Hindus, has existed since
the creation of the world. The rajas and their subjects lived
there from the earliest times and spoke their own *bhaka* (dialect).
A thousand years ago, the Muslims became the masters there.
Mahmud of Ghazni was the first, and after him the Ghurs and
the Lodis became the rulers. This led to an intermingling of
the languages of the Hindus and the Muslims. Finally, Amir
Timur (in whose family the empire remains to this day)
conquered India. As he camped with his troops in the city, its
bazar or marketplace came to be known as *Urdū*. Then after
the establishment of Mughal rule Humayun, distressed at the
hands of the Pathans, went to Persia. When he returned and
punished the troublemakers, no mischiefmonger remained to
create any disturbance; the empire prospered.

When Akbar ascended the throne, people from all parts of
the country were attracted towards his capital because of his
patronage and liberality. They spoke different languages and
dialects. But now that they were together and had to converse
with each other in the ordinary business of life, a common
language was born in the city streets.

When Shahjahan Sahib Qaran got the Red Fort, the Jama
Masjid and the city walls erected and the Peacock Throne
studded with precious stones installed in a tent made of gold
and silver brocade pitched on poles, and when Nawab Ali
Mardan Khan built a canal to Delhi, he (Shahjahan) was much
pleased. He held celebrations and made that city his capital

and it came to be known as Shahjahanabad. (Although the old city of Delhi is distinct from it, yet that is called the old city and this the new). He gave the name '*Urdū-e-Mu'allā*' to the bazar of Shahjahanabad.

Thus from the time of Amir Timur until the reign of Muhammad Shah and even to the time of Ahmad Shah and Alamgir II, the empire remained undisturbed generation after generation in the same family and, in the course of time, the Urdu language became so chiselled and refined that the language of no other city could match it. Nevertheless, one should be impartial to appreciate and judge it; otherwise, who conceives his headgear, dialect and behaviour to be improper? If you ask a countryman, he censures the city idiom and considers his own to be the best. But then, only the learned ones know which is correct. After a long time, God has sent one such learned and discerning man in Mr John Gilchrist who, with his profound knowledge and insight and immense labour and research, compiled books of grammar. The language of Hindustan became common throughout the country and got a new elegance and flourish.

A city flourishes from the prosperity of the king. When Ahmad Shah Abdali came from Kabul and got the city of Delhi pillaged, Shah Alam was in the eastern parts of the country. There was no one to look after the city and so it was destroyed. The nobles of the city too had to leave and take refuge where they could. Wherever they settled, their idiom got impure when they interacted with the local people. Then there were many others who happened to go and stay for a few years in Delhi. How can they too speak the pure languages of the city? Sooner or later they are bound to make an error. But the person who suffered great misfortunes and floundered about like a piece of stone in the streets of Delhi where five to ten generations of his family have lived, one who saw the court of the nobles and participated in the fairs and religious congregations, and who even after leaving the city kept his language uncorrupted, his and his language alone will be pure and correct. One such, this humble being, has arrived here (Calcutta) after seeing every city and witnessing every spectacle.

The Beginning

Now the tale. Please listen and deal justly with it. Thus it is, as written in *Qissa-e-Chahār Darvesh*, and as it is told.

Once upon a time there ruled a king in Turkey, as just as Naushervan and as benevolent as Hatim. His name was Azad Bakht and his capital was Constantinople (Istanbul). Everyone was happy under his rule. The treasury was full, the army well off and the poor at ease. Every day was festive and every night full of joy. No thefts and robberies took place as thieves, robbers, pickpockets, swindlers and mischiefmongers were banished from his kingdom. Nobody shut the doors of his house or shop at night. The travellers who passed through his kingdom went safe with their silver or gold.

He was a great king ruling over a thousand cities and many a ruler and overlord paid him the annual tribute. Yet he was a God-fearing man. He never neglected his duties or his prayers to God. He had all the pleasures and comforts but no son and this worried him constantly. After his daily prayers he prayed to God to bless him with a son who might be like a lamp in his dark abode, carry on his name and ascend the throne after him.

He reached his fortieth year and this remained his cherished hope. One day, after he had said his prayers, he was passing through his crystal palace when he happened to see his image in one of the gilt-edged mirrors. To his dismay, he saw a white hair, glittering like a silver wire in his beard. His eyes were filled with tears and a sigh issued from his heart. 'Alas,' said he to himself, 'all my life has gone to waste. I oppressed the

1

people for things mundane. What use are all these big countries I have conquered and the heaps of gold and precious stones I have gathered in my treasury? I see my 'death so very near. Even if I live for a few years more I will only grow weaker day by day. Perhaps it is so destined that I should have no son to inherit my throne. I must die one day and leave all these things to no one. I am now fairly advanced in age; it is better for me to quit them now and devote the rest of my life wholly to God.'

Having resolved thus he came into the palace garden where all his court members were assembled. Ordering all others to go he made his decision known to his ministers and the nobles of the court. He ordered them to assemble only in the Hall of Public Audience and to look after the affairs of the kingdom themselves and not to disturb him any more.

He then retired to his private chambers. For days and days together he remained there and kept lamenting and praying to God and observing fasts. He would break his fast only with a date and three mouthfuls of water, barely sufficient to keep his body and soul together. Nobody dared disturb him. He prayed to God night and day.

By and by all his people came to know that the king had secluded himself. Thus there was confusion and turmoil in the kingdom. Mischief-makers and evil-doers raised their heads. Corruption became the order of the day and rebellions broke out. The nobles of the court assembled to discuss this state of affairs. None of them had the courage to go to the king and request him to reconsider his decision. At last they went to the grand old vizier, Khiradmand the Wise. They respected him very much as he, more than anyone else, had been in the confidence of the king. They related to him the state of affairs and said, 'If this continues, the entire kingdom will be lost.' Khiradmand the Wise replied, 'Though the king has forbidden us to disturb him, yet let us take a chance. We should all proceed together and humbly request him to kindly reconsider his decision.' He took them all with him. Leaving them in the Hall of Public Audience, he proceeded to the Hall of Private Audience and sent word through the royal page to the king that, 'This old servant is in waiting and humbly seeks Your Majesty's favour to grant me presence. It is long since I have had the honour of seeing Your Majesty. Kindly allow me to kiss your feet.'

The king recalled to his mind the services of Khiradmand the Wise and ordered that he be called in. He was conducted to the private apartment of the king. He bowed low in respect to him. He saw that the king had grown weak; his face was pale and his eyes had sunk into their sockets. He could not restrain himself. Devoted to the king and his father as he had been, he was moved to see him in that state. He threw himself at his feet and wept. The king helped him to his feet and said, 'Now that you have seen me, do not disturb me any more. Go and leave me alone.'

But Khiradmand did not leave. With tears rolling down his cheeks and his beard he said, 'What is it, Your Majesty? Why have you thus secluded yourself? This sudden withdrawal of Your Majesty from public affairs has led to utter chaos in the kingdom. Kindly recall what pains Your Majesty's ancestors took to build it? Your Majesty's seclusion will ultimately bring it to ruin. Why is it that Your Majesty has so resolved? If Your Majesty will be pleased to let it be known, this humblest servant may be of some help. After all, what are we servants for if we cannot at least partake of our master's troubles and do all that we can to bring him comfort?'

The king said, 'That is all right, Khiradmand. But my sorrow is such that no one can help me. I have now grown old. My death is so very near; this hoary head of mine reminds me of it. And you know I have no son who may take my place after me. This makes me sad and so I have renounced it all. I am no more interested in retaining my kingdom; nor do I bother about my riches. Enough of this world I have seen! It's of no use. I wish to go to some far off lonely mountain, away from this fretful life. In the woods I shall retire and pass the rest of my life praying to God. Thus alone may I hope for a better life when I pass away.' He then heaved a sigh and became silent.

Khiradmand the Wise had been the vizier to the king's father as well and had held the king dear to his heart ever since he was a prince. He said, 'To despair of God is not just. One who has created eighteen thousand worlds by uttering one single word, can it at all be difficult for him to bless you

3

with a son? May Your Majesty be pleased to banish such thoughts from your mind, or else the empire which your ancestors took great pains to build will be lost in no time. There will be utter confusion and chaos and, God forbid, you will leave behind a bad name. And then you will be censured on Judgment Day and held responsible for it in the eyes of God. Even your prayers here will not bring you any good there. Man's heart is the seat of God and you know a king will be judged by his justness and good deeds to his subjects. Pardon me, Your Majesty! To leave home and wander about in the woods is the way of hermits and those who have renounced the world. It does not become a king. You are a king and ought to behave like one. Worship and devotion to God does not rest on becoming a recluse or retiring to the woods and mountains. Your Majesty may have heard this verse:

> God is always with man
> But man seeks Him in the wilderness;
> The child is well in your arms
> And you search for it in the city.

'Kindly consider what I say. Always keep God in mind and pray to Him. No one has ever been disappointed in His grace. In the morning attend to the affairs of your kingdom, dispensing justice to all; help the poor and the needy so that they may live in peace and pray to God for your prosperity. At night you may say your prayers and invoke His blessings on the pious ones. Feed the orphans and the prisoners, the poor and the destitute, and the widows every day. If God wills it so, such good deeds will help you win His favour and you will get your heart's desire fulfilled and be happy. Have confidence in God's grace. He can accomplish in a moment what He wills.'

The king felt relieved to hear these words of sincerity. He said, 'Be it so, Khiradmand; let me do as you say. God's will alone be done! What have the other nobles and ministers been doing?' Khiradmand said, 'All the nobles and ministers are concerned about Your Majesty's welfare and pray for your prosperity. At the moment they are in the Hall of Public

Audience. Would Your Majesty be pleased to let them have the honour to see Your Exalted Self and thus comfort them?' The king said, 'Not just now, Khiradmand. I will hold a general court tomorrow; tell them all to attend.'

Khiradmand was quite happy at this. He raised his hands and blessed him thus: 'As long as this earth and heaven exist, may Your Majesty's throne and crown remain!' Then he took his leave. He came to the nobles and ministers. He gave them the good news and informed them of the king's wish that all of them and the citizens attend court the next day. They were relieved and left rejoicing in the good news. The whole city rejoiced.

Early the next day all the nobles and ministers, and the citizens, came to the court and took their seats. The king then appeared to the beat of drums and sat on his throne. All of them bowed in respect and laid before him the presents they had brought according to their ranks. They were rewarded by the king accordingly. Every one was glad that he had again started to call his court and attend to the affairs of the kingdom himself. At midday he dismissed the court and went into his palace. There he partook of the royal repast and retired to rest.

Thereafter, the king held his court in the morning and in the afternoon he would peruse some religious book or say his prayers to God to fulfil his heart's desire after repenting over his sins and craving mercy from God.

One day he happened to read in a book that 'one who is afflicted with grief and feels helpless, should submit himself to Fate, visit the tombs and pray to God to bless his soul for the sake of His Prophet and should always fear Him; he should always remember that he is nothing before Him and that there have been countless powerful kings and monarchs who passed away from this world; as is so aptly said:

Seeing the moving handmill
Kabir wept and said,
'Alas, no one has survived
The pressure of the two millstones

5

(Of the heavens and the earth).

They left all their mighty empires and pomp and show behind them and but for a handful of dust no trace remains of their existence. Nobody knows about them or about what happened to them after their death—what insects ate them up and how they fared with God. Thus alone shall one realize that this world is a transitory place and man has nothing to gain from it; it is a puppet show. Thus alone shall one find peace.'

The king found the passage highly significant. He found in it an echo of what Khiradmand the Wise had said to him. He decided it was divine guidance for him and resolved that at night he would pray to God or present himself before the holy men who lived in seclusion so that he might get what he desired in this world and deserve deliverance in the next.

And so one night, without telling anyone, he left his palace in disguise. Outside the city he went and in a short while reached a cemetery. It so happened that a mighty storm broke out just then. Roaring violent winds began to blow all around. But the king was firm in his resolve. To his surprise, he saw at a distance a flame, bright like a morning star in that cemetery. 'How is it,' he wondered, 'that a flame remains unextinguished in such a storm? Is it a talisman? Or has someone sprinkled alum and brimstone around its wick to sustain it? Or is it some holy spirit which makes it burn? Whatever it is, let me go and find out. Maybe this very light kindles the lamp of my house and by its grace my heart's desire is fulfilled.'

As he went nearer he saw four dervishes, all wearing the dress of the dead and sitting quietly against each other with their heads on their knees. The king could not see their faces but by their postures he felt that they were afflicted with grief. They seemed like dead figures on the wall. An earthen lamp placed on a stone and untouched by the stormy wind shone brightly near them as though shaded by the heavens. A pot of fire also lay nearby. Azad Bakht was somehow convinced by this sight that his desire to beget a son would be fulfilled if those saintly persons prayed to God for him, and that the dry tree of his hope would revive and bear fruit if they attended to it. Still, before joining or greeting them he thought it would be better for him to make sure that they were not some evil spirits in the garb of men. So he hid himself quietly in a corner wherefrom he could see them more clearly and hear them if they talked to each other.

There was profound silence when by chance one of the four dervishes sneezed and then said, 'Praise be to God!' The other three dervishes raised their heads from their knees. One of them trimmed the wick of the lamp. All of them lit their hookahs from the pot of fire nearby and began to smoke. One of the dervishes, after some pulls at his hookah, said, 'Friends, we have wandered long and seen many ups and downs in life. We are all in misery but know nothing of each other. Praise be to God! By some strange stroke of luck we are brought together. We know not what will happen tomorrow, whether we will remain together or go our separate ways. The night is telling on us and it seems early to retire. It will be better if we start narrating, without any exaggeration, the stories of our lives. We may thus talk out the night. We shall just lie down here when a quarter of it remains.' The other dervishes said, 'It's a good idea. God be our guide. First you kindly tell us how you fared in life. We shall certainly profit by it.'

Adventures of the First Dervish

The first dervish sat at ease. Looking towards the sky he heaved a sigh and said, 'With your permission, friends, I relate the story of my life:

> Listen now all, what went with me!
> Listen, how the heavens tossed me up and down!
> Listen, what vicissitudes countered I;
> Listen as I relate them all!

'I was born in Yemen, my native place. My father, Khawja Ahmad, was the biggest merchant in the country. He had agents in many parts of the world. He had many a warehouse full of merchandise of all sorts. Large sums of money in cash, and silver and gold were always at hand. He had only two children—my sister and myself. She lived with her husband, a merchant's son, in another city. I was brought up in affluence and with much delicacy. I learnt reading and writing and the military science and bookkeeping.

'But fate had something else in store for me. When I was fourteen my parents passed away. This was an unexpected blow which left me an orphan with no one to look after me. I was struck with profound grief and I mourned their death day and night. On the fortieth day of mourning my relatives assembled to perform the last rites of my dead parents. They prayed for their souls and consoled me. 'Know it, dear,' they said, 'losing one's parents is the heritage of man. Every one has to die one day. Whatever your father has left is yours now.

8

You are the master of it all and now it is your duty to look after it well and carry on your business with utmost care and diligence.' After thus consoling me they left. All my agents and employees too came to me and offered their condolences. They requested me to take charge of the cash in hand and the goods in stock.

'I wondered at the huge amount of wealth my father had left. I took charge of it and started living my own life. My drawing-room and private apartments were elegantly furnished with the choicest things: costly furniture, beautiful curtains and apt fittings. Things for merrymaking were provided as well. Handsome servants clad in rich liveries were employed as my personal attendants and I would relax reclining against cushions in my drawing-room. Considering me a boy of tender age, sychophants and knaves and such others did not take long to gather around me. They talked idly and kept me in good cheer and through their counsel wine and women too were introduced in our midst. And I was happy to indulge wildly in them. Man, as you know, meets the devil in man. In their company I devoted myself to the pleasures of the flesh and lavishly spent my father's money on women and wine and in gambling. The result of neglecting my business was obvious. Even the proverbial treasures of *Korah* would not have sufficed my extravagance. Wealth got without effort is ill spent. So it was not long before I found that I had spent all that my father had left me. My servants left me. And those false friends disappeared too. Even if I chanced to meet them, they turned their eyes from me. Penniless and friendless, and with nothing to eat, I wondered where to go and what to do. I began to look like one dying of starvation. Completely dejected, I thought of going to my sister. I was much ashamed since in my life of comfort and leisure I had not even replied to any of her letters after our parents' death. But I could not think of anywhere else to go.

'And so, although conscious of my shamelessness, one day I started on foot and after an arduous journey reached my sister's place. She was shocked to see me in that wretched condition. She burst into tears and cried, "What ill luck has befallen you, my dear brother?" Guilt, on account of my behavour in the past, did not allow me to utter a single word. She was all kindness. She distributed alms to the poor for my safe arrival and sent me to the bath. She got me new clothes and arranged for me a separate elegantly furnished apartment near her own. Good breakfasts and wholesome meals twice a day restored my health. I thanked God; He had given me comfort after such hardship. But it was not to last for long.

'One day my sister said to me, "Thank God! He has given you a new life. I would never wish you to remain away from me. But you know it is a strange world. It is every man's duty to work. What will people think of you if you sit idle at home? They will say that after spending all your father's wealth you are now living on your brother-in-law's charity. And this will be a sad reflection on our parents. I feel now is the time you should start doing something." "I myself would like to," I said, "but you are now like my mother; I shall do as you please."

'She was pleased to hear this and went to her apartment and soon reappeared. With the assistance of her maidservants she brought fifty bags of gold sovereigns which she placed before me and said, "I understand that a caravan of merchants is to leave for Damascus in a day or two. You should join it. Take this money and purchase whatever goods you can sell at a profit in Damascus. Find a merchant honest enough and entrust your goods to him. Meanwhile you too should go to Damascus and take the proceeds from the sale of your goods from him when he arrives there. Whatever merchandise remains you may sell it yourself at a profit."

'I took those bags of gold and went to the wholesale market of general merchandise. Fortunately, I met one of the merchants of the caravan. With his counsel I bought the goods and entrusted them to him and got a receipt as my sister had advised. I went back to my sister and told her what I had done. She was pleased.

'Two days later the merchants set off by sea. I took the overland route. My sister provided me with a good horse and put some eatables for me in a leather bag. she tied a sacred rupee on my arm and marked my forehead with curd to guard against evil on my journey. With tearful eyes she said, "God be with you! May you remain safe and return soon." Thus she bade me farewell.

'I mounted my horse and set out for Damascus. The weather was fine and the horse well-bred. It did not take me long to reach there. But since it was already night, the city gates had been closed. The guards did not concede to my request to open the gates so that I might enter the city. I, therefore, alighted from my horse and spreading my saddle-cloth on the ground, sat down. A mysterious silence prevailed there. I could not sleep and just walked up and down. When it was midnight, I saw a big chest tied with strings being lowered slowly down the city wall. I was quite amazed at this. "Is it a talisman?" I said to myself, "or perhaps, God Almighty has taken pity on me and sent me an unexpected treasure in this big chest." When it reached the ground I grew impatient to know what it contained. I went near it. It was a wooden chest and when I opened it I could not believe what I saw. There lay a beautiful woman in it. She was wounded and the blood stains on her clothes were not yet dry. Her eyes were closed and from her face it appeared that she was in extreme agony. The sight struck me dumb. She slowly moved her lips and said, "O cruel wretch, is this how you repay all my kindness and affection? Well, you may give me yet another blow. I leave it to God to do us justice." I just wondered and in a thoughtless mood found myself uttering these words: "I cannot understand who the devil could have ever thought of injuring such a fair lady. And she still remembers him in this death-agony." Upon these words she opened her eyes, drew the veil from her face and looked at me. Our eyes met for a moment. That glance of her's pierced through my heart. I nearly fainted. But somehow I mustered enough courage to ask her, "What is it? Tell me, please, who are you and who treated you thus?" She had not the strength to speak. Only faintly she said, "Thank God! But my wounds do not allow me to speak. I might live only for a few moments more. When I have breathed my last, please be kind enough to bury me in this chest at a place where nobody may find it. And thus I may escape the condemnation of the people. May God bless you for this!" Then she became silent and pulled her veil over her face.

'I put the chest near my belongings. I was determined to help her. But I too was helpless. I had to wait till dawn. Those remaining hours of night were really too long and heavy for me. At last the day dawned. I heard the cock crow and the cry of the muezzin from the mosque inside the city. I said my morning prayers, put the chest on my horse and as soon as the gates opened I entered the city. I asked the people where I could get a house on rent. With great difficulty I found a comfortable house. The first thing I did was to take that fair lady out of the chest and make her a soft bed. I found myself a trustworthy servant who told me of a good barber-surgeon, well versed in the art of surgery. Leaving the lady under his care I went out. After ascertaining it from people, I searched for and found the place of the surgeon, Eisa by name. He was an old man with a flourishing beard, sitting at his door. A few men were preparing powders and plaster materials beside him. I paid him my respects and said, "I came to this city for trade and brought my wife along with me out of my love for her. On the way when night set in I did not think it advisable to proceed further. We stayed under a tree. When it was past midnight we were attacked by robbers. They wounded my wife and took away all her jewellery. I was helpless since they were too many. Early this morning we entered the city. She has grown very weak. I have rented a house and left her there. God has given you such great skill in the art of surgery. I have heard much of your renown and have come to seek your help. Would you kindly come along with me and save her life? I shall be ever grateful to you for this favour."

'Eisa was really a kind-hearted man. He took his bag of medicines and came along. After examining her he said, "She is severely wounded but she will be all right within forty days if God wills it so." He washed the wounds in neem-water. He stitched some of them, put bandages on others after applying some ointments and said, "I will come every morning for dressing. Please see to it that she has complete rest, lest the stitches give way. Give her chicken soup in small quantities and musk-water to keep her strength." With these instructions he took his leave. I presented him a bottle of rose scent and said, "May God bless you! You have given me new hope of her life." In my heart I prayed for her health, never left her alone and saw to it that she had complete rest as advised.

Meanwhile, the merchant of Yemen to whom I had entrusted my goods also arrived there. I took my goods from him and sold them in the market at whatever price they fetched. The proceeds thereof I began to spend on her. The surgeon visited her every day and dressed her wounds. In a short time her wounds healed. When she recovered completely and took her bath of health, I thanked God and presented a robe of honour to the surgeon. I was extremely happy, as though I had got the kingdom of the seven realms. I celebrated the occasion and ordered costly colourful carpets to cover the floor and got a cosy and elegant seat for her with soft cushions and pillows. There she sat—so beautiful, her face bright like the full moon and eyes sparkling as if to dazzle me. I distributed a huge sum of money among the poor. I kept myself at her service and did what she asked me to do. One day, in her vanity, she said, "Look, if you want my pleasure, always do what I say; never try to meddle in my doings, or else you will repent." Nevertheless, from her looks it appeared that she was grateful for my kindness and services to her. I would do nothing without her approval and obediently did whatever she asked me to. Months passed in this manner, yet I never knew the mystery behind her nor had I the courage to ask her about it.

'I realized that my resources were fast depleting and that it would not be long before I had spent my last penny. The thought distressed me much because I was a complete stranger there and knew no one to seek help from. One day she guessed my distress from my face and said, "Look here, man, whatever services you have rendered me, I shall never forget. At present I am unable to pay for them. But if you require anything for the day to day expenses, bring me a piece of paper and pen and ink." From her behaviour I presumed that she must be a princess, or else she would not have addressed me thus nor would she have spoken with such confidence. I gave her a pen, some ink and paper. She wrote a note and handing it over to me said, "By the three arched gates near the fort, you will find a big mansion in the adjoining lane. The master of that house is Sidi Bahar. Go and deliver this note to him."

'I followed her instructions and soon found the place. Through the door-keeper I announced my arrival. No sooner had he reported it in the house, than a handsome and pleasing young negro, wearing an attractive turban, came out to see me. He said nothing but politely took the note from me and went in. Within a few moments he came back, followed by slaves who carried on their heads eleven trays covered with silk cloth. He ordered them, "Go with this young man and deliver these trays." I took my leave of him and went to my house with those slaves. Dismissing them at the door I took those trays in and placed them before the fair lady. She looked at them and said, "Keep these eleven bags of gold sovereigns with you to meet the day to day expenses." I took those bags but the mystery deepened for me and I became more disturbed. "It is really strange," I said to myself, "that a person unknown to me should give me so much money at the sight of a short note, without asking me any questions. I cannot ask the lady for she has already forbidden me to inquire about anything." So I grew more anxious and lost my peace of mind.

'Eight days later, she said to me, "God has bestowed on man the robe of humanity which does not get torn or soiled. Worn out clothes do not diminish his stature and humanity, yet a man in such clothes seldom commands respect in society. Take some money and go to the market and buy two elegant suits and some jewellery for yourself from Yusuf's shop."

'I mounted my horse and went to the shop described. I saw there a young man in saffron-coloured clothes. He looked really handsome. Many a passer-by would stop to have a look at him. I greeted him and mentioned the articles I required. He knew from my accent that I was a foreigner and said, "You can get all you need here but tell me please where you hail from and the purpose of your visit to this country." I did not think it proper to relate to him my story. So I avoided it somehow and collected the dress and jewellery and paid its price. As I rose to take my leave, he was displeased and said, "If you wished to keep the mystery about yourself, why did you display such warmth at first?" He sounded upset and I thought it uncultured to take my leave abruptly. I sat down. He was much pleased at this and said, "Many thanks, Sir, for this kindness! Would you also favour me with your company tonight? I am inviting some of my friends and hope we shall have a good time." As I always had the fair lady on my mind and had never left her alone nor had done anything without her consent I made many excuses. But he would not let me leave until he had extracted a promise from me to attend the party.

'So I went back to her and placed the articles before her. She asked their price and inquired about the jeweller. I told her of his invitation and of my acceptance of it provided she approved. She said, "Our Prophet said we should accept such offers of hospitality. Since you have given your word, you should keep it. Leave me under the protection of God and keep your promise." I said, "As a matter of fact, I do not wish to go and leave you alone, but now I must carry out what you say. I shall go but my heart will be here with you."

'I went back to the merchant and found him waiting for me. "Welcome, sir," said he, "you have kept me waiting for long." He took my hand and led me into a garden. It was really delightful there with fountains playing in the basins, canals rippling and the trees laden with various kinds of ripe fruits. Birds of many species were twittering in the trees. There was a grand pavilion in the centre of the garden and each apartment was elegantly furnished. We sat down in a beautiful saloon by a canal. After a while he left and presently returned in another rich dress. On seeing him I said, "What a beauty! May God save you from an evil eye!" He said, "Better if you also change." To please him I did. He had managed well for my entertainment and provided for everything required for the occasion. He kept me warm company and his conversation was quite charming. Meanwhile, a cup-bearer appeared with a crystal cup and a flask of wine. Many delicacies were also served. We had had a few rounds of the sparkling wine when four young beautiful boys with their flowing tresses entered the saloon and began to sing and play. So delightful and absorbing were their songs that even Tansen would have forgotten his strains and, like Baiju Bawra, been driven to distraction on hearing them. While we were so absorbed, my host, the young merchant, with tears rolling down his cheeks, said, "Now we are good friends; and as no religion approves of keeping a secret from a friend, I frankly confide a secret in you. I have a mistress. With your permission, may I send for her here and thus exhilarate my heart with her presence? I cannot fully enjoy these pleasures without her." He spoke so fondly of her that I too became anxious to see her. I said, "I only wish your pleasure. Nothing better than what you propose. In fact, there is no true enjoyment without one's beloved. Without any further delay, you may, please, send for her." The merchant made a sign towards the screen which was placed there and presently came in a black woman, as ugly as a witch. She took her seat by him. She was so ugly that one would die on seeing her without even being claimed by death. I was really frightened to see her and thought, "Is it really possible that this ugly woman is the beloved of such a handsome young man? And, is she really the one he had praised so much and so fondly spoken of?" However, I just cursed him for his taste and said nothing.

'For three days and nights together we enjoyed the music and wine. On the fourth day I was exhausted and fell asleep. The merchant woke me up in the morning and after giving me a few cups to shake off the hangover said to his beloved, "Now, to trouble our guest any more is not fair." Hand in hand, we stood up. I begged my leave. With great warmth he bade me farewell. I put on my dress and left for my place. I had never before stayed out of my house at night, leaving the lady alone. So I hesitated to face her after the absence of three days. I offered my apologies and told her all about the festivities and the merchant's insistence on my keeping him company. As she knew the social etiquette she said, "Well, it doesn't matter. You did the right thing. One can't leave unless the host permits. But after having enjoyed the feast and the festivities there, will you let it be at that? Won't you invite him to a feast in return? You should go to the merchant and bring him with you and treat him with hospitality twice as great as his. Do not worry about the means; everything will be easily arranged for and in a grand manner by the grace of God."

'So I went back to the merchant and said to him, "I accepted your invitation and enjoyed your hospitality. Now you too must give me an opportunity to entertain you." He politely said, "I am entirely at your service, my friend." I said, "It will be a great honour if you come along with me to my place now."

At first he was reluctant, but on my insistence he agreed. I took him to my place. But all the time on my way back I thought of my poor circumstances, saying to myself, "Had I the means, I too would have entertained him in a grand manner. I do not know what sort of a treat he is going to have." Absorbed in such thoughts, I reached near my place with him. I was surprised to see the great bustle and preparations for a reception at the door. The street had been swept clean and sprinkled over with water. The guards with their clubs in hand stood alert. I wondered at this but since I knew it was my place I entered it. What I saw there puzzled me all the more. Rich carpets were spread in all the apartments; and there were big cushions, betel and scent boxes, flower vases, containers of rose-water to shower over the guest and silver spittoons—all properly placed. On the niches were placed crystal chinaware of different colours and shapes. On one side of the hall lamps glowed behind a bright screen of mica; on the other side they were arranged in the shapes of cypresses and lotuses. In the hall and the balcony camphor candles were lit on golden candlesticks, and glass shades studded with jewels were placed over them. Attendants stood in waiting. Some of them were busy cooking in huge pots in the kitchen. Fresh small earthen pitchers wrapped in clean fine cloth with small earthen pots on them were placed on silver stands in the water-chamber. There were also covered mugs and big cups set in ice and saltpetre to cool the water therein. They were nicely arranged in big round dishes on a low table.

'In short, everything for a royal feast had been nicely arranged. Dancing girls and boys, musicians and entertainers, all gaily dressed, stood ready to perform. I took the merchant along with me and got him seated by a big cushion in the centre of the hall. I was surprised to see that all those arrangements, made in such a short time. I looked for the lady but could not find her. As I went into the kitchen, I saw her in another apartment. Her head covered with a white scarf and in a simple dress and ordinary slippers, she was busy supervising the arrangements for the feast. Though unadorned, what a beauty she was:

Those on whom God beauty hath bestowed

Indeed, no ornaments do they need;
Though unadorned, beautiful they remain
Like the full moon uneclipsed!

She was giving the cooks directions to prepare various dishes and make them as tasty as possible. In fact, she, with her rose-like delicate frame, was all asweat because of that toilsome work. I went to her and invoking blessings of God on her I tried to flatter her and admired her good sense and understanding in making arrangements for the feast. She said, "Man can do what even angels cannot. What is it that you so admire? Enough of this flattery; I do not like it. Tell me what etiquette is this that you have come here leaving your guest all to himself? What will he think? Go and attend to him. Send for his mistress too to give him company."

'I went to the merchant and entertained him. Meanwhile, two handsome servants carrying flasks of wine and cups studded with precious stones entered and started serving us. I said to him, "I am sincerely at your service, my friend. It will be proper, if with your permission, the beautiful lady you love so much also joins you here. I may send a man to bring her, if you please." The merchant was overjoyed to hear this and said, "Ah, my friend, this is just what I had in my heart." So I sent a eunuch to bring her. It was midnight when that ugly witch arrived in an elegant palanquin like an unexpected evil. To please my guest I received her with all respect and got her seated by him. He was so delighted on seeing her, as though he had been given all the pleasures of the world, and the devilish fiend, too, eagerly embraced him. Verily, it seemed that the bright full moon had been eclipsed. All those present there gaped in wonderment and said, "See what an evil is cast on this young man!" With such a ludicrous sight before them, they forgot all else and stared at the couple. One of them remarked, "Friends, love and reason are opposed to each other. This accursed love may see what reason can never conceive. Try to see Laila with the eyes of Majnun." All those present exclaimed, "True, true indeed!"

'I devotedly attended to my guest as my lady had advised. However much the merchant urged me to share drinks with him, I refrained from drinking on the pretext of my duties as a host. Actually I feared lest I should earn the displeasure of my lady. Nor did I take interest in the amusements there. Three days and nights we passed like that. On the fourth night the young merchant said to me, "I must now beg my leave; out of love for you I have neglected my work and been here for three days. Pray, won't you sit now for a moment and share the pleasures with us?" I thought he would feel hurt if I did not. Besides, good manners do require one to please a friend and a guest. So I said to him, "I am obliged to give in, my friend. Courtesy demands I should care more for your commands than for my duties as a host." He offered me a cup of wine which I had to take. Then we had several rounds more at a stretch, with the result that in a short time all those present there lay dead drunk. I also fell unconscious and woke only when it was morning and the sun was high up.

'I looked around and found that all the crowd had vanished. Nor could I see the lady. The house was empty except for a bundle wrapped up in woollen blanket in corner. When opened, it revealed, to my horror, the headless bodies of my guest and his mistress. This horrible sight unnerved me. I was shocked and struck dumb. I could not understand what had happened. I just wondered and looked around, when I happened to see the eunuch who had helped prepare for the feast. Seeing him I was comforted. He exclaimed, "What is the use of knowing all about it now?" I agreed with him in my heart. However, after thinking over it for a while I said, "Well, you may not speak about it but do tell me where the lady is?" He replied, "Of course, I will tell you whatever I know but pray tell me how does it behove a sensible man like you to get dead drunk without the permission of my lady and that too with a man whom you came to know only a few days ago?" These polite words made me realize my mistake and I said, "Indeed, I committed a folly; pardon me, please." The eunuch all the more kindly gave me the lady's address and bidding me farewell went to bury the two dead bodies. Thank God, I had nothing to do with that horrible event.

'I was anxious to meet the lady. It was only in the evening that I could locate her residence with great difficulty. I passed the night in great anxiety sitting in a corner near the gate. I did not hear any footstep, nor did anybody bother about me. I sat there helpless and neglected. When it was morning and the sun had risen, the fair lady chanced to look at me through a window. Only my heart knows how I rejoiced. I thanked my stars. Meanwhile, a eunuch came to me and said, "Go and stay in the adjoining mosque; there you may get what you want." I went to the mosque as advised but my eyes were still fixed at her door and I wondered what the future had in store for me. I passed the whole day and waited for the evening with the anxiety of a person who observes a fast from early in the morning till the sun sets. At long last the evening set in and the day, heavy like a mountain on my heart, came to pass. The eunuch who had given me the lady's address came to the mosque. He was a kindly person and kept all the secrets of the lady. He comforted me and took me along with him into a garden. He asked me to sit there and said, "Stay here until you get your heart's desire." He then took his leave, probably to convey my good wishes to the lady. I tried to amuse myself with beautiful flowers in full bloom, the bright moonlight and the fountains playing in the basins. But the roses reminded me of her rose-like beauty and the full moon brought her fair face to my mind. Without her, all those delightful things pierced my eyes like thorns. At last, I saw her, bright like the full moon, at the garden gate. Richly dressed and in a fine embroidered veil she stood there, a few steps away from me on the garden path. Her very presence revived the beauties of the garden and filled my heart with joy. She sat down beside a bright big cushion in a lavishly adorned alcove. Like a moth that goes round a candle, captivated by the flame, I presented myself before her and stood there like a slave with folded arms. The eunuch pleaded for me. To him I said, "I am guilty, indeed, and I should be punished for it." The lady, much displeased, arrogantly said to the eunuch, "The best thing for him now is to take a hundred bags of gold, pack up and go back to his country." On hearing these words my spirits fell. All seemed dark before me. Out of despair I heaved a sigh and tears flowed from my eyes. None else but God was my hope. In despair I said, "Will you kindly think it over? Had I sought worldly gains, I would not have so recklessly spent in your service whatever little I had. Isn't there any consideration for devotion and selfless service in this world that you look so displeased with me? If so, I see no charm in life now. Love and unfaithfulness cannot go together." These words offended her much. She grew more indignant and with derision said, "Ah, so you claim to be my lover! Indeed, has the frog then caught a cold? You fool, don't forget who you are! It's no more than a mere fancy. Stop this nonsense. Never utter such words again! I swear by God, had any one else dared thus, I would have had him cut to pieces and thrown before vultures and kites. But alas, I still remember your kindness to me! I repeat, even now the best thing for you is to return to your country. Only thus far had fate decreed your lot with us!" With despair in my heart and tears in my eyes I said, "If it is so ordained that I should not get my heart's desire and if I am destined to wander about in the woods and over mountains, I feel I am helpless." Showing disgust at these words she said, "I cannot abide such flattering silly words. Better go and find someone else who is worth it!" Still enraged, she got up and left. However much I tried to beseech her she paid no attention to what I said.

'Disappointed and frustrated I also left the place. Thereafter, it became my routine to wander about the city-streets and retire to the woods only to come back and wander about the streets again as though I had gone mad. Forty days I passed in this manner without food in the day and rest at night. Like a washerman's dog I wandered from pillar to post. Man remains alive only if he takes food and water; he is just a worm which lives on food. As I did not eat or drink anything, I lost all my energy. Like an invalid I lay under the wall of the mosque when the same old eunuch came to say his Friday prayers. He happened to pass by me when I was reciting this verse in a feeble voice:

Give me the strength to bear this aching heart,
Or else give me death;
Whatever is destined for me, O God,
Let it befall soon!

21

'It was difficult to recognize me by my face; so weak and pale had I grown. He recognized me by my voice and was moved to see me in that condition. Looking intently he said, "So, this is what you have made of yourself." I said, "Whatever was destined has come to be; whatever little I had, I spent on her; and now I lay down even my life for her. If she wishes it so, what can I do?" On hearing these words the eunuch left a servant with me and went into the mosque. When he returned he carried me in a litter to the lady's house where he got me seated behind the screen in her apartment. Changed I certainly was yet she should have had no difficulty recognizing me, having known me for a fairly long time. But she pretended not to know me at all and asked the eunuch, "Who is this fellow?" The kindly man replied, "This is the same unfortunate man who has earned your displeasure. That is why he is in such a pitiable condition. The flame of love is burning him. The more he tries to put it out, the more fiercely it burns. Moreover, he is dying of the shame of his folly." She laughed at this and said, "Why tell me lies? I remember receiving reports of his having reached his country long back. God knows who you are talking of." The eunuch folded his hands in respect and said, "If you kindly grant me leave, may I say a few words?" She said, "Say whatever you have to." The eunuch said, "You are a better judge. For God's sake, please let this screen be removed; you will not fail to recognize him. Take pity on him. To ignore the facts is not just; add to your good deeds. It will be disrespectful if I say any more. Pray, do as you please, which will be the best." She smiled faintly and said, "Well, who is attending here? Keep him under medical care and bring him to me when he gets well." To this the eunuch said, "You yourself shower some rose-water on him, please, and say a kind word to him. That alone will revive him with a new hope of life. On hope alone rests the world." Even then the lady refused to say a kind word. Disgusted at this I mustered up courage and said, "I do not wish to live in this state any more. With one foot already in the grave I care too little about my life to fear losing it. It is up to the princess now to pull me out. She may, or she may not; it is entirely her sweet will." At last, God, who controls feelings, softened her heart. She became

kind and said, "Quick now, send for the royal physicians."
Presently they came and after carefully feeling my pulse and
examining my urine said, "This man is certainly in love with
someone. Unless he has his beloved in his arms he will not
recover." These words of the physicians convinced her of my
love. So she at once ordered, "Take this man to the hot bath,
dress him properly and bring him to me." I was carried out,
given a bath and taken to her in a proper dress. She politely
said, "You have brought me a bad name for nothing! Come
now; what else do you want me to do?"

'O dervishes, my joy knew no bounds at these words. In
fact, I was so overjoyed that I feared I would die. I said, "Praise
be to God! At the moment you have done more than what all
the science of medicine could do; your words have given me
a new life. Just notice the change your kindly words have
brought about." Uttering these words, I went round her three
times and said, "As you bid me speak out what I have in my
heart, I wish you to give me a place at your feet which I hold
as more precious than the kingdom of the whole world." For
a while she became thoughtful. Giving me only a sideways
glance she said, "Now take your seat. Your services and fidelity
are indeed such that you may say whatever you please. They
are engraved on my heart. If you so wish I have to accept."

The same day, at an auspicious hour under the sign of an
agreeable star, a qazi was called who performed the marriage
rites. After so much trouble God showed me the happy day
and I got what I wished. But much as I desired to get the fair
lady, I was also anxious to know all about the strange events
that had taken place. Even now I knew nothing about the
handsome negro who had given me so many bags of gold on
just seeing a short note. Likewise, so many other things still
remained a mystery: the instant grand feast, the gruesome
murder of the guest couple, her casting me away and now this
sudden favour ending in our marriage. In fact, my anxiety to
unravel the mystery of all those events was so great that in
spite of my fondness and love for her, I could not bring myself
to share the bed with her. For eight days and nights I remained
with her without consummating the marriage.

'One morning, when I asked one of the maids to prepare

the bath for me, my wife smiled and said, "Really, do you think you deserve a hot bath?" I kept silent but she was surprised at my conduct. In fact, I could read anger on her face. At last one day she said to me, "You are a strange man! What is this? You showed so much warmth before but now you are so cold. If you had not the powers why at all did you wish this?" I boldly said, "Darling, try to be just. Justice is what everyone should observe." She said, "What more justice do you want? Whatever you wished has come to be!" I replied, "Verily so, I got what I had earnestly wished for. But I have been troubled and a man in such a state of mind cannot accomplish anything. I had determined that after our marriage, which was of course my heart's delight, I would request you to kindly explain the mysterious events that have baffled me. Only then will I be at ease." The lady was furious at this and said, "Excellent, isn't it? Too soon you have forgotten what I had told you. Just try to recall how many times I have asked you not to meddle in my affairs or seek explanations. Why do you take this liberty then?" I laughed at this and said, "As you have allowed me greater liberties than this, can't you forgive this one too?" My words brought a sudden change in her. She was like a whirlwind of fire. Full of rage she said, "You take too much liberty now. You should mind your own affairs. What will you get out of such explanations?" I said, "The greatest shame in the world is to expose the parts of one's body which modesty requires to be covered. But if life is to continue one has to lay aside this feeling. Now that you have allowed yourself to me, why keep any secrets from me?" She knew what I meant. Becoming peaceful she said, "True, but I am afraid lest it may bring us trouble." I said, "Why worry about this? Please trust me and relate all the events of your life. I won't speak of it even to myself." When she felt convinced that I would not be satisfied unless I knew all about her life and that the blind man's buff could not go on, she said, "This may indeed cause us great trouble. You are foolishly insisting on knowing it. But since it is your pleasure I should seek now, I have to relate all the events of my past life. But be careful and keep it between you and me and the lamppost." After impressing it on me in so many words she said, "This unfortunate being before you is the daughter of the king of Damascus who is greater than all the other sultans. I was his only child and was brought up in luxury with love and care by my parents. As I grew up I became unnaturally attached to beautiful women. I kept lovely young girls of my age and of noble families in my company. Pretty maids were always in my attendance. I enjoyed their dance and music and led a carefree life. I praised God for this. But gradually it so happened that I felt myself changed within and I lost all interest in the company of others. The gay assembly gave me no pleasure. I was restive, sad and confused in my heart. Nothing seemed to please me, nor did I like to talk to any one. Finding me gloomy and sad, my maids felt much concerned and begged to know the cause. This faithful eunuch has always kept my secrets. Nothing in my life has ever been concealed from him. Finding me in a deep melancholy, he said one day, 'If the princess takes a little of the exhilarating drink she may get well and become cheerful again.' When he said this I was inclined to take it and ordered him to bring it for me. He went out and returned accompanied by a young boy bearing a nicely prepared goblet cooled in ice. I drank it and found that it really did me good, as the eunuch had said. I bestowed on him a rich robe of honour and ordered him to bring one such cup at the same hour every day. The boy regularly brought it and I drank it. It exhilarated my spirits and in inebriation I would start jesting and playing with the boy and enjoying myself. The boy became much too familiar and his respect for me wore off. He would amuse me by telling pleasant stories. He was wonderful when mimicking the affectations of women. He was handsome and I found my attraction towards him growing and I gave him presents every day. But to my astonishment, he was always clad in dirty beggarly clothes. One day I said to him, 'What is this? You have received so much money from me and still you come in the same dirty dress. Do you spend all the money I give you or do you just save it?' Finding me so interested in him, he said with tearful eyes, 'My master takes all that you kindly give me. He does not leave a single penny with me. How, then, can I make new clothes and come well-dressed before you? I am helpless.'

'"The boy's humble submission and poverty made me all the more generous to him. There and then I asked the eunuch to look after him, give him good clothes to wear and bring him up under his care and to see that he did not mix with idle boys. I made it clear to him that I wanted the boy to be properly brought up and to become worthy of my company. The eunuch, finding me so interested in the boy, faithfully carried out my orders and took every care in bringing him up. And thus it was not long before the boy wore a good appearance and like a snake cast off his old slough. Much as I resisted, his beautiful form made me so fond of him that I always wanted him to remain with me and I wished to hug him to my breast. At last I made him my companion. I would dress him in rich clothes and jewels and keep him before me for hours and hours together. Thus did I comfort my aching heart. I saw to it that he got what he wished. I felt restless when he was away from me. In a few years he grew into a fine youth and the down appeared on his lips. Now the servants would take note of his presence and the guards objected to his entering the female apartments. His visits were thus discontinued. But I could not live without him. Every moment of his absence weighed heavy on my heart; it seemed as if I was facing death itself. I was restless, for I could not even speak of it to anyone, nor could I bear his separation from me. O God, what would I do? Sadness sat heavy on my heart. I called my eunuch who had kept all my secrets and said to him, 'Look here, I wanted the boy to be brought up well and to flourish. I propose now that he be given a thousand gold sovereigns so that he may have a jeweller's shop in the market and live well. Buy him a well-built house near my residence. Get him servants and slaves and fix their pay so that he may live in all comfort and ease. The eunuch established for him a jeweller's shop and got him a well-furnished house and whatever else was needed. In a short time his shop was the talk of the place. Rich clothes and robes of honour and precious jewels and other things required for the king and the nobles could only be had from him. By and by the choicest things of every country were available there. The business of all other jewellers became dull. In short, no other jeweller could match him in the city, nor in any other country. Thus he made a great fortune. But his separation from me was telling on my heart. I could not think of any plan to meet him and comfort myself. So I again took my eunuch into confidence and said to him, 'I cannot think of any plan to see him and comfort myself except that an underground passage be made from his house to my apartment.' Immediately work was started and in a few days the passage was ready. So, every day, as the evening set in, the eunuch secretly conducted the young man to me and for the whole night we remained together and enjoyed ourselves. Both of us were divinely happy when together. When the morning star appeared and the muezzin called the people for the morning prayers, the eunuch led him by the same underground passage to his house. No one except the eunuch and the two maids who had nursed me in my childhood knew about this.

'"We passed fairly a long time in this way. One day the eunuch went to call him as usual to my apartment. Finding him sad he asked, 'Is all well? Why do you look so sad? Come along, the princess has sent for you.' The youth made no response. The eunuch came back and reported it to me. Possessed by the devil as I was, I continued to think of him with love. Had I known that love for such an ungrateful one could ruin me and bring me a bad name and that I would lose my honour and respect, I would have controlled myself and taken a vow not to think of him any more, let alone remain devoted to him. But, alas, it was so destined. I ignored his shameless attitude and regarded his disobedience as affectation and airs of a lover. The result is that you too have come to know of all that has happened. Disregarding his mulish attitude I sent him this message through my man: 'If you do not present yourself here just now I shall come there and you must know that this is fraught with danger. If it leaks out, it will be disastrous for you. Do not behave in a way which may bring us nothing but disgrace. Better you come here rather than force me to come to your place.'

'"From the message he knew that my love for him was unbounded and he came assuming airs and in a disagreeable mood. When he sat down by me I asked him, 'What is it that makes you so disturbed and cold today? Never before have you been so disrespectful. You always obeyed me.' He said, 'I was poor and an unknown person. By your kindness and help I have amassed so much wealth. I live very comfortably and pray for your long life and prosperity. Please forgive me for my misconduct. Most humbly I beg your pardon.' As I really loved him, I accepted his apology in good faith and did not suspect any evil design on his part. With even greater affection I asked him, 'What is it that disturbs you so much? Just say it and it shall be solved.' Humbly he said, 'Everything difficult for me is easy for you.' From his roundabout talk I gathered that an elegant garden with a grand house in it in the heart of the city near his residence was for sale, and that with the garden a female slave, who was a good singer and well-versed in music, was also to be sold. But it was a package deal, like a cat tied to a camel's neck. Whoever purchased the garden would also have to buy the slave; and, strangely enough, the price of the garden was only a hundred thousand while the price of the slave was five hundred thousand. He humbly said, 'I am unable at present to spend so large a sum.'

'"Thus I discovered that he had set his heart on them, for even though he was in my presence he looked gloomy and sad. As I always wanted to see him happy, I at once ordered the eunuch to get the sale deeds completed in his name and to pay the amount from the royal treasury the next day. The young man thanked me and his face brightened. We passed the night as usual, enjoying each other's company. In the morning he took his leave. The eunuch faithfully carried out my orders. He bought both the garden and the slave for him. The young man continued to visit me at night and leave in the morning as usual.

'"One day in the rainy season, the clouds were hanging low and it was drizzling. Lightning flashed through the dark clouds and a pleasant breeze was blowing. It was so delightful. As I saw the display of wines of various colours in flower-shaped glasses nicely arranged on the niche, I was tempted to take a draught. After drinking two or three cups, thoughts of the newly purchased garden came to my mind. I thought of visiting it for a while. As they say: 'When misfortune comes, the dog bites the camel rider'. Taking a female servant with me I went to the young man's house through the underground passage from where I proceeded to the garden. It was really a delightful place, like the proverbial Garden of Eden. Drops of rain on the green leaves shone like pearls set in emerald; red flowers against the low-hanging clouds presented a sight as that of the crimson red of the sky when the sun sets. The canals, full of rippling water, glistened like a floor of glass.

'"I strolled about in the garden till the day came to an end and the night set in. It was then that I saw the young man taking a stroll. When he saw me, with all respect and warmth he came near and, taking me by my hand, led me towards the pavilion. As I stepped in, I found that its beauty far excelled the elegance of the garden itself. The illumination was superb. The lights were so well-arranged—there were many lamps arranged in the shape of cypresses and some were lotus-shaped; some were placed in beautiful chandeliers with their branches holding the lights while there were others with decorated shades, placed in an assembly. All of them had been lit. There was so much brightness that even the *Shab-i-Barat* with its full moon and illumination would have appeared dark before it. Fireworks of numerous kinds were being displayed.

'"Meanwhile, the bright moon emerged from behind the dispersing clouds like a lovely mistress dressed in lilac. This made everything all the more delightful and as the moonlight spread the young man said to me, 'Let us now go to the balcony of the pavilion.' Like a fool I did whatever the wretched fellow proposed. He led me upstairs. I found the balcony was so high that all the buildings and the street lights could be easily seen from there. With my arm around his neck I sat there enjoying the sight when an ugly woman came to us with a flask of wine in her hand. I was displeased to see her. Rather alarmed at her sight I said to the young man, 'It seems a strange affliction! Who is she?' Folding his hands in respect to me he said, 'This is the slave girl bought with this garden by your kindness.' I realized then that the fool had set his heart on her. I was much displeased and felt indignant but said nothing. But that rascal did much more to annoy me. Imagine, he had the audacity to make that unworthy woman the cup-bearer for me! I was, indeed, like a parrot caged together with a crow. Neither did I wish to stay there nor had I the opportunity to leave. The wine was so strong, it could make a beast of man. She served him two or three cups of that fiery drink at a stretch. Willy-nilly I also gulped down half a cupful on his insistence. In short, that shameless unworthy woman got drunk and started taking liberties with the young man. That mean fellow too got intoxicated and started to behave unbecomingly. I was so ashamed that I wished the earth to split at that moment and gobble me up. But so crazed was I in love for him that even then I said nothing. A vile wretch as he was, he did not think much of my forbearance. Already intoxicated, he drank two cups more and lost whatever little sense he had. He forgot all about respect for me and began to behave more indecently. Completely intoxicated, the impudent villain indulged with that ugly woman in my presence. And she too, the hideous one, lay there with all her female airs and affectations. As they say: 'Like priest, like people'; the two were well-matched; he was as ungrateful as she was shameless. I felt so out of place that I cursed myself for having gone there and brought this upon myself. It was perhaps a proper punishment for my folly but how long, after all, could I put up with it? I was on fire from head to foot, as though rolling on burning coals. My presence there reminded me of the proverb, 'The pannier jumped without the ox, whoever saw such a paradox?' So I got up to leave the place. He guessed his ruin in this. Perhaps he dreaded the consequence if I felt offended. So he thought of killing me if he could. Having thus resolved in his mind and taking that shameless woman into confidence, he put his girdle round his neck as a sign of submission and fell at my feet. Putting his turban at my feet and with tears rolling down from his eyes he humbly begged of me to forgive him. Because of my infatuation for him he made me do whatever he liked. In fact, I was like a handmill in his hands and he turned me as he wished. I had no will of my own. So I was easily persuaded to take my seat. He filled two more cups of that fiery wine and induced me to drink as well. The strong wine soon made me completely senseless. And then, that cruel ungrateful fellow wounded me with his sword and thought I was dead. On receiving the wounds I opened my eyes and said, 'Well, I got what I deserved. But save thyself from the consequence of unjustly shedding my blood:

Wash the stains of my blood from thy clothes
Lest some cruel one take hold of thee!

What is done is done; do not reveal our secret relationship to anyone. I have not spared even my life for thee.' Thus wishing him mercy of God I lay unconscious and knew nothing of what happened thereafter. Perhaps that callous man thought me dead and put me in the chest and let it down over the city wall where you found it.

'"I wished no one ill; yet such misfortune was in store for me. Nobody can rub off the lines of one's fate. My eyes were the cause of all this. If I had not taken a fancy for that handsome ungrateful fellow, he could not have become the cause of my ruin. God so ordained that you reached there and saved my life. I am so ashamed of all this disgrace that I wish to live no more, or at least to hide myself from everyone. But how can I? One cannot choose even one's own death. I was almost dead but God gave me life anew. Let us see what fate has in store for me now! Apparently your kind attention and care did me good and I recovered from those deadly wounds. You spent on me whatever you had. When I saw you worried because you were short of money, I wrote the note to Sidi Bahar who keeps my accounts. I had written that I was safe and had asked him to inform my kind mother of my unfortunate circumstances and whereabouts. He entrusted you with those trays of gold for my expenses. Then I asked you to purchase jewellery and rich clothes from Yusuf, the merchant. I knew that the poor fellow made friends with everyone and would certainly try to make friends with you as well and, due to his boastful nature, would probably invite you to a feast. My conjectures proved right. He did what I had thought; on your return after making a promise to him you told me of his insistence. I was pleased at this for I knew if you accepted his invitation you would also like to invite him in return and that he would be only too eager to oblige. So I quickly sent you back to him. After three days when you returned and made apologies for your absence I said, 'Doesn't matter; I know you could not come unless he would let you. But not to be equally courteous and remain indebted to him is not fair.' So I asked you to go to him and extend a return invitation. When you left I realized that there was little to entertain him at our place if he happened to come along with you. Luckily, it is the custom of the kings here to go on tour for eight months in a year to look after the state of affairs in the country and collect the revenue. They stay in the capital only during the four rainy months. The king, that is the father of this unfortunate being, had gone on a tour of the country at that time. Sidi Bahar had told the queen, my mother, of my unfortunate circumstances. Before you returned with the young man I, although deeply ashamed of my behaviour, got the time to present myself before her and tell her all that had happened to me. Wondering about the consequences of my disappearance, she kept it a guarded secret out of motherly affection and foresight. She had concealed my sins in her maternal breast. Nevertheless, she had all along been worrying about me. As I told her all about my disappearance and the ill treatment I had suffered, she was full of tears and said, 'You unfortunate being! You have scarred royal honour and glory. A pity, that you have ruined your fair name too. Better if I had brought forth a stone than you, my daughter. Even now you should repent; whatever was written in your fate has come to be. What are you after now? Will you live or die!' Much ashamed of myself I said, 'It was so ordained in my fate that I should live in disgrace and distress even after such adversities. Better if I were dead! I may have earned a bad name, but I don't think I have done any such thing which may bring disgrace to my parents. What pains me is that both those shameless persons should go unpunished and enjoy themselves. What a pity if I cannot punish them! I request that Your Majesty's steward be ordered to make arrangements for a feast at my house so that under the cover of a feast I may punish the two for their evil deeds and thus avenge myself. I will cut them to pieces as he had so callously wounded me. Only then will my thirst for revenge be quenched, otherwise its flames raging within me shall reduce me to ashes.' With these words, my mother, out of maternal affection and love, sent all that was needed for the grand feast, including the attendants, under the supervision of the eunuch. In the evening you returned with that mean villain. I wanted his shameless harlot also to be there. So I pointedly asked you to send for her. When she came and all of you assembled together, they drank plenty of wine and became intoxicated. You too lay dead drunk with them. I ordered their heads to be cut off. The armed woman guard drew her sword and cut off their heads then and there, leaving their bodies bathed in blood. I felt angry with you because I had permitted you to entertain them and not to get drunk with persons you scarcely knew. Indeed, I was not at all pleased with this folly of yours because how could one expect faithfulness from one who had intoxicated himself ignoring all other considerations? But I am so bound in gratitude to you that I cannot but forgive you.

'"Now you know every fact from the beginning to the end. Do you want any more explanations? As I have done my part I wish you to do yours. I think it is no longer proper for you or for me to stay in this city. But, of course, now it is entirely at your discretion."

'God be praised! The princess thus narrated her story. As I held her sweet will to be above everything else and was deeply in love with her, I said, "As your gracious self is pleased to propose, I will do all that you wish me to do and without hesitation."

'Impressed by my sincerity and faithfulness the princess advised me to get two strong and swift horses from the royal stable and keep them ready. I picked up two such horses, got them saddled and brought them to our house. When a few hours of the night remained, the princess, disguised as a man, armed herself and mounted one of them. I also armed myself and mounted the other horse, and we set out. By the evening, as darkness fell, we reached the banks of a big lake. Alighting from our horses we washed ourselves, hurriedly took a little food, mounted again and set off. Now and then the princess would say, "For your sake, I have sacrificed my honour and left my parents and country and all my wealth. Now you too may not behave with me like that ungrateful and cruel one."

Sometimes I talked of different things to pass the time as we rode on. I tried to allay her doubts and said, "Know it, my princess, that all men are not alike. He must have been low of birth. That is why he behaved as he did. I have spent all that I had on you and to you I have devoted my life. You have done me honour in every way. I am now just like a slave without the purchase price and will not utter a word of complaint even if you wish to make shoes of my skin and wear them." We passed the time in such conversation and on and on we went night and day. At times, feeling tired, we alighted from our horses. We killed birds and animals in the woods and striking a fire with our flints, roasted them and ate them with the salt we had with us and let the horses out to graze.

'One day we reached a vast open land where there was no trace of habitation. No human being was to be seen. Even at such a desolate place the day was festive and the night full of joy to me because I had the princess with me.

'We went on and on till we came to a mighty river, the sight of which would sink the firmest heart. As far as we could see there was water and more water. There seemed to be no limit to it. O God, how could we cross it? We just wondered when it occurred to me to leave the princess there and go in search of a boat. The princess could also rest in the meantime. I said to her, "My dear, with your permission I may go and find some way to cross this mighty river." She said, "I am so tired; hungry and thirsty too. Let me rest while you look for some means to go across." There was a huge pipal tree nearby whose expansive crown could shelter a thousand riders from the sun and rain. Leaving her there under the tree I set out to look for anyone on land or on the river. Long though I searched, I found no trace of a human being.

'When I returned I did not find the princess there. How can I describe the state of my mind at that moment! I lost my senses and became almost mad. In that very condition I climbed up the tree and looked for her in the branches and leaves, then fell to the ground and went round and round the tree, weeping and wailing and raising a heartrending cry over my misfortune, then running from east to west and from north to south. I ran all over to find her. In vain I searched for the rare pearl I had lost. In helplessness I wept and threw dust over my head and looked for her everywhere. I thought some jinn had carried her away or else someone from her country had followed her and, finding her alone, persuaded her to return to Damascus. So disturbed was I by these thoughts that I returned to the city, threw my clothes off and like a naked fakir wandered about the streets of Damascus from morn to eve in her search. At night I would lay myself down wherever I could. I wandered about here and there and everywhere but found no trace of my princess. Neither did I hear anything about her anywhere, nor could I discover the cause of her disappearance. So, thinking that my life was useless without her, I climbed up a mountain with the intention of throwing myself over the cliff so that I might end my miserable life. I was just about to throw myself down when someone held me by my arm. I turned around and found a veiled rider in green clothes saying to me, "Why do you wish to end your life? Only infidels despair of the mercy of God. So long as there is life, there is hope. Three dervishes who are distressed and have seen the vicissitudes of life like you have will meet you soon in Turkey. The king of that country is Azad Bakht. He too is distressed. When he meets all four of you, the wishes and desires of each one of you will be fulfilled." Holding the stirrup and kissing it I said, "O friend of God, your very words have consoled my afflicted heart, but for God's sake, tell me please, who are you?" He said, "I am Murtaza Ali and to extricate those who are in difficulty is my job." Saying these words he disappeared from my sight. Thus, after taking comfort from the happy news I received from my master (Ali), the Remover of Difficulties, I made up my mind to leave for Constantinople. To fulfil my wish of meeting the princess I suffered all the misfortunes destined for me. By the grace of God I am here now and it is my good fortune that I have met you. What remains now is that we meet Azad Bakht, the king. Only then will the desires of all five of us be fulfilled. Pray then, and say "Amen!" O God, our Guide! This is what happened to me and I have related it to you. Now let us see when my sorrows and troubles due to the loss of the princess are changed into joy and happiness."

Azad Bakht, who had hidden himself in a corner, heard with great attention the adventures of the first dervish and now prepared himself to listen to the adventures of the second one.

Adventures of the Second Dervish

Now it was the turn of the second dervish to tell his tale. He made himself comfortable and said:

> 'Friends, listen now the story of this faqir;
> I relate it from beginning to end.
> It's a pain no physician can cure;
> Listen, please!

'At present we are all clad in worn-out clothes; but I want you to know that this humble being is a prince of Persia where one can find the most learned. That is why Isfahan is called half the world. No kingdom in all the seven climes is equal to it. The sun, which is the greatest of the seven constellations, is the zodiac-sign of that land and rules its destiny. The climate there is delightful and the people intelligent and cultured. I was just a boy when my father, the king, appointed the most accomplished people in every field as tutors to teach me statecraft so that I might be truly educated. By the grace of God I completed my education when I was fourteen. I was well mannered and learnt the art of polite conversation and all that a king should know. I enjoyed being in the company of learned people and listening to stories of adventurous kings and famous men of every land.

'One day the one who was well-versed in history, said, "Though man cannot count much on this life, yet he may have certain qualities that bring him name and fame to last till the Day of Judgment." I said to him, "Please tell me about such qualities in detail so that I may try to cultivate them in me."

He, thus, related to me the adventures of Hatim Tai: "There was in the time of Hatim a king in Arabia named Naufil. He grew jealous of Hatim, who had earned a good name for himself. One day, he took his army to fight a battle against Hatim, a pious and God-fearing man. Hatim thought that if he joined the battle, the creatures of God would be killed as there would be much bloodshed and he would be punished by God for it. So he ran away and hid himself in a cave in the mountains. Naufil confiscated all his property and proclaimed publicly that whosoever brought Hatim to him would receive five hundred gold sovereigns as a reward. News of this reward made people greedy and they began to search for him.

"'One day an old man and his wife with two or three of their children happened to be near the cave where Hatim had hidden himself. While they were collecting wood the old woman said, 'If we had any luck we would have found Hatim and taken him to Naufil. He would have given us five hundred gold sovereigns and we would have lived in comfort and been rid of this fret and toil.' The old man said, 'What are you talking? Perhaps it is so destined that we should pick wood everyday, carry it on our heads and sell it in the market and thus survive, or else a lion will devour us one day. Well now, do your work. Why should Hatim fall into our hands and the king give us so much money?' The old woman heaved a sigh and kept quiet.

"'Hatim heard them talk like this. He thought it unmanly and uncharitable on his part that he should hide for his life and not provide that poor family an opportunity to fulfil their desire. A man without mercy is not a true man; and one who has no feelings is like a butcher indeed:

Man was created to show compassion
Otherwise, the angels were not wanting in devotion!

"'Hatim's goodness did not let him remain in hiding any more. He came out of his hiding place and said to the old man, 'My friend, I am Hatim. Take me to Naufil. On seeing me will give you the money as he has announced.' The old man said, 'True, it will be to my advantage to do so but who knows what treatment he will accord you. If he puts you to death, what shall I do? No, this I am not going to do. I shall not take a man like you to your enemy for my own benefit. How many days shall I enjoy the promised wealth? And how long shall I live? At last I have to die one day. How then shall I face God? Hatim implored him much and said, 'Take me to the king; I say it of my own free will. I have always wished my life and property to be of use to someone.' But the old man did not agree to take Hatim to the king and claim the reward.

'"Hatim was disappointed at this and said, 'If you do not take me to the king as I say, I will go to him myself and tell him that you had hidden me in a cave in the mountains.' The old man laughed and said, 'Well, if I get evil in return for my goodness, it is my hard luck.' While they were thus talking to each other, some passers-by gathered round them. When they learnt that it was Hatim, they at once caught him and carried him off. The old man followed them full of grief. When they took Hatim before Naufil, he asked who had caught and brought him there. A mean-faced, hard-hearted fellow boasted, 'Who else but I could have done this job? In my name has been written this chivalrous act! I have raised the standard of glory to the heavens!' Another boaster came forward and blurted out, 'I searched for him for days and days together. I caught him in the woods and brought him here. Please think of my labour and grant me the promised reward.' Thus, out of lust for money, everyone claimed that he had done the job. The old man stood alone in a corner, hearing the tall claims of these persons. He wept for Hatim. When all of them had said whatever they had to say of their 'act of chivalry and enterprise,' Hatim said to the king, 'If you ask for the truth, let me tell you. The old man standing there, away from the others, has brought me here. If you are perceptive you will realize this is the truth and reward him for catching me as you have promised. The tongue alone is most valuable in the whole body, and a man must always keep his word; otherwise if God had given tongues to brutes as well, what would have been the difference between a man and an animal?'

'"Naufil called the old woodcutter to him and said, 'Tell me the truth. Who has caught Hatim and brought him here?' The poor man related to him all that had happened and said, 'Hatim has come here of his own accord for my sake.' Naufil was highly surprised to learn of this noble act of Hatim's, and said to him, 'How generous of you! You did not care even for your life for the good of others!' He ordered that the hands of all those who had made false claims be tied behind their backs and they be given five hundred strokes of a shoe on their heads instead of five hundred gold sovereigns and then be discharged. They received the punishment there and then till they became bald. Truly, it is sinful to tell a lie and no sin is worse than this. May God keep everyone away from this sin. Many people go on telling lies but repent when caught and punished.

'"After thus punishing them, Naufil thought, 'It is unmanly to kill or bear enmity towards a man like Hatim. He is entirely devoted to God and does not spare even his life for the sake of the needy and poor. Thousands of people benefit from him.' With great warmth of feeling and friendship he held Hatim's hands and said, 'Of course, why would it not be so! Only a man like you is capable of such nobility.' With due respect he offered Hatim a seat by him and restored to him his leadership of the tribe of Tai and ordered five hundred gold sovereigns to be given to the old man from the Royal Treasury. The old man invoked blessings of God on the king and took his leave."

'When I heard this story, I felt ashamed and said to myself, "Hatim was just a chief of a tribe, and he is still remembered for his generosity; I am the future king of all Persia; it will be a pity if I haven't the good fortune to earn at least that much fame. As a matter of fact, nothing is better than generosity in this world, for, whatever man gives in this world he gets much more in return in the next. It is like reaping much more than you sow." With these thoughts I called for the Master of Works and ordered him to build a grand palace with forty high and wide gates to it outside the city as soon as possible. In a short time it was ready and there I distributed coins of gold and silver to the needy and poor every day from dawn to dusk. Whosoever begged for alms, I granted it to his fill. In short, those in need entered the gates and were given whatever they wished for.

'One day a fakir came in through the front gate and begged

for alms. I gave him a gold sovereign. He returned through another gate and begged for two sovereigns. I knew it was the same person but I put up with it and gave him two. In this way he kept on coming through each gate and each time he begged for one sovereign more. I played ignorant and gave him as much as he asked for. At last he came in through the fortieth gate and asked for forty sovereigns which were accordingly paid to him. Even after receiving so much, the fakir came in again through the first gate and again begged for alms. I had had enough and said to him, "Look, you greedy man, what sort of a fakir are you that you don't even know what the three letters of the word *'faqr'* (a life of poverty with resignation and content) stand for? A true fakir should observe and live up to them. He said, "Well, you the benevolent one, please explain them to me." I said, "The letter *fe* stands for *faqah* (fasting), the letter *qāf* for *qana'at* (contentment), and the letter *re* for *riyazat* (devotion). One who doesn't have these qualities in him is not a *faqir*. Spend the huge amount given to you, and when it is all spent you may again come to me and take whatever you need. These alms are given to meet your needs and not to hoard. O greedy man, you received one sovereign more every time you returned and you came back forty times. Just add them up and see how many sovereigns you have got; and even after receiving so much, your lust for money has brought you back again through the first gate. What will you do with so much money? A *faqir*, truly so described, ought to think only of the passing day with the firm belief that God, the Great Giver, is always there to take care of him the following day. You should be ashamed of yourself and be patient and content. What sort of resignation and contentment is this that your master has taught you?"

'The fakir got annoyed and, throwing all the money before me, said, "Enough sir, do not be too angry; take it back and keep it with yourself. But never again think that you are generous. You cannot afford to be. You are still far from it, and you simply cannot reach it. Know ye, that the word *sakhi* (generous) too has three letters signifying three things; practise them first and then let yourself be called a generous man." I felt uneasy and said, "Well, holy man, please explain them to me." He replied, "The letter *sin* stands for *sama'i* (tolerance); the letter *khe* stands for *khauf* (fear of God) and the letter *ye* signifies *yad* (to remember that one who is born has to die one day). Unless one has these traits in him one should not aspire to be called a generous man. The generous man is held so high in esteem that even if he be an evil-doer he is dear to God. This humble being has travelled through many lands but none except the princess of Basra can be really called generous. To her measure alone God has cut out the robe of generosity. All others wish to be known as generous but they do not live up to it." Much I beseeched the fakir by all that was sacred to me to kindly forgive me and take whatever he wished but he did not take anything and went away saying, "Now even if you give me all your kingdom I would not even spit on it."

'The fakir went away but I lost my peace of mind after hearing so much praise of the princess of Basra and wished to go there and see her.

'In the meantime the king, my father, passed away. I ascended the throne and the empire passed on to me. But thought of the princess of Basra did not leave me. I consulted the vizier and the nobles who were the pillars of my kingdom and said to them, "I propose to make a journey to Basra. Carry on your duties steadily in my absence. If I remain alive, I will return in a short time." No one agreed with me on my proposed journey. I was sad and helpless. One day, without consulting anyone, I secretly sent for the resourceful vizier and appointed him my agent to look after the state's affairs. Putting on a saffron-coloured robe like that of a fakir, I set out all alone and after a few days I reached Basra. Wherever I stayed for the night, the officials readily welcomed me and provided comfortable houses for my stay. They served many varieties of food and remained in my attendance all night. At every stage of my journey I received the same hospitality. In such comfort and ease I travelled for months and finally reached the city of Basra. No sooner had I entered the city than a well-dressed, cultured and handsome young man came to me and said, "I am here only to serve travellers. I take every one of them to my house, be it a fakir or a merchant. Visitors to this city stay with me. Please do me the honour and stay with me." I asked him his name. He said, "This humble one is known as Bedar Bakht." Impressed by his excellent manners and politeness I went with him to his house. It was a grand mansion furnished in royal style. He led me to an apartment where he made me sit. He ordered warm water for me and got my hands and feet washed. Then the food-cloth was spread and the table laid. There was a great variety of food and fruits and sweetmeats and confectionery. * Seeing so many dishes laid before me on the table, I felt I had already had enough. Partaking a little from each dish I was soon full. The young man said, "How little you have taken, sir! The table is as it was, untouched. No formality, please, have some more." I said, "No question of formality in taking one's meals! May you prosper ever more! The food is really delicious and I relished it. Now, pray get it set aside." When the food-cloth was removed, a gold-bordered velvet cloth was spread and an ewer and a basin of gold full of warm water was brought. He got my hands washed with scented gram flour.

'Betels and betel-nut and cardamoms wrapped in silver and kept in a jewelled box were served. Whenever I asked for water to drink the servant brought it cooled in ice. When the evening set in, camphorated candles were lit in glass shades. The sweet young man was with me throughtout to entertain me. When a quarter of the night had passed he pointed towards a richly prepared bed with a canopy and said, "Now, sir, you may kindly take rest." I said, "But for us poor fakirs a mat or a hide is enough; these luxuries God has ordained for men of the world like you." He replied, "All these are meant for fakirs and dervishes like you; they are not for me."

'He insisted, so I went to the bed and found it softer than rose-petals. Flower vases and lit incense sticks stood on either side. In this euphoric state I fell asleep. In the morning, almonds, pistachio-nuts, grapes, figs and other dried fruits and fruit juice were served at the breakfast table for me.

'Thus I passed three days and nights there. On the fourth day when I begged leave of him he folded his hands in respect

---

* Here the author lists thirty three dishes and seven kinds of bread.

to me and said, "Perhaps I have not served you well. That is why you seem to be so displeased." A bit surprised, I said, "For God's sake, what are you talking? The norms of hospitality require one to stay at a place only for three days. So I have stayed here. It won't be proper if I stay here any longer. Moreover, I am a traveller. It is not right for me to stay long at one place. As such, I beg to leave although one would not like to leave this place after all your kindness and hospitality." He said, "As you please, but just a minute so that I may go and inform the princess. And now as you propose to leave, I request you to accept all that is here in this guest house. These beddings and gold and silver utensils studded with jewels are your property now. Arrangements will be made so that you may carry them with you." I said, "Do not talk of it, please; as if I am a beggar and not a fakir! Had I any greed and lust in my heart why should I have become a fakir? I would have remained a man of the world." The young man said, "When the princess comes to know of your refusal she may discharge me from her service and God knows what other punishment she may give me. If you do not accept them, please lock them up here in a room under your seal and then proceed, as you please."

'I would not agree and he would accept no refusal. At last it was decided that all those articles be locked and sealed in a room. Then I prepared to leave. But in the meantime a highly placed well-dressed eunuch with a gold wand in his hand and followed by a retinue of good-looking servants wearing their proper insignia came there and addressed me politely, "Dear Sir," he said, "it will certainly not be beyond your kindness to do me the favour of visiting my humble place and thus exalting me by your gracious presence there. Otherwise God knows what punishment the princess may give me when she learns that a traveller came here and left without anybody receiving him well. In fact, it will be a blot on my very life." I did not want to accept his invitation. But he persisted and took me to a house, much bigger tham the first one. Like my former host he also treated me for three days in the same grand manner, serving rich food and fruits, and told me that I was the master of all the gold and silver utensils and carpets and furniture in the house and that I was free to dispose of them as I pleased.

'I was all the more surprised at this and wished to escape from there somehow. He guessed it and said, "O man of God, let me know what you want or aspire for so that I may humbly convey it to the princess." I said, "In this garb of a fakir, how can I wish the riches of this world that you offer me without my asking for it and which I refuse?" He remarked, "No human heart has ever forsaken the wish for worldly things. As a poet says:

> *I've seen fakirs with nails uncut,*
> *I've seen fakirs with long locks of hair;*
> *I've seen fakirs with ears split*
> *And their bodies covered with ash;*
> *I've seen them, their heads shaved,*
> *And tongue-tied as if they were dumb;*
> *I've seen those enjoying themselves,*
> *And those who live in the forest;*
> *I've seen the brave and the chivalrous,*
> *I've seen the wise and the ignorant,*
> *I've seen the rich given to their riches;*
> *I've seen those who are always happy*
> *And those who have suffered all their lives;*
> *But I haven't seen one*
> *Who has no lust in his heart!"*

'On hearing this I said, "True, but I want no such thing. If you permit, I may write a note containing my heart's desire which you will please present to the princess. You will thus do me a favour as if you bestowed all the riches of the world on me." He said, "With great pleasure! I see no harm in it." I wrote a note beginning with the praise of God. Then I related my circumstances and wrote, "I am a humble being and came to this city a few days ago. I have been very well received and looked after by Your Majesty's officials. I had heard much of your goodness and generosity. But I find that they far exceed what I had heard. They now advise me to write down for your kind perusal what I wish. I say, then, without any inhibition, what is in my heart. I do not want the riches of this world as

44

I am myself the king of my country. It was only because I had
an ardent desire to see you that I came here all alone in this
condition. I now earnestly hope that by your kindness my
heart's desire will be fulfilled. But then, it depends entirely on
your sweet will. I may only submit that if this humble request
is not granted I shall continue to wander as I have done and
like Majnun and Farhad I shall lay down my life which knows
no peace in this passion."

'I gave the note to the eunuch who carried it to the princess.
After a short while he came back and conducted me to the
door of the seraglio. There I saw a respectable old woman
wearing costly jewellery. She was sitting on a small golden
stool and many eunuchs were standing in her attendance with
folded arms. I took her to be the chief of the female-servants
and paid my respects to her. She politely returned my salutation
and said, "Most welcome, please take your seat. Is it you who
wrote the fond note to the princess?" I just blushed and kept
silent, lowering my head. After a short pause she said, "Young
man, the princess has acknowledged your greetings and ordered
me to convey to you that 'there is nothing wrong in my taking
a husband. You have asked for my hand but you say you are
a king. To think of yourself as a king in this beggarly state of
yours, and to take pride in it are quite out of place; for, you
should know that all men are equal among themselves though
more respect is due to those who hold the Islamic faith. I have
also thought of marrying for a long time. You are indifferent
to the riches of the world as you say; to me also God has given
so much of it that it cannot be taken account of.' But before
marrying her," the old lady said, "you must first fulfil one
condition, if you can." I said, "I am prepared to accept it; I will
not spare my wealth or life. Pray, tell me the condition!" The
old lady said, "Wait, tomorrow I'll let you know." With pleasure
I accepted it. Then I took my leave and came back.

'I was restless the whole day. When the evening set in, a
eunuch called on me and took me with him into the palace.
The nobles and learned ones were present there. I also took
my seat. In the meantime dinner was served and they invited
me to join them. After dinner a female-servant came out of the
seraglio and said, "Where is Baharvar? Call him here." The

attendants immediately conducted him there. He looked respectable. Keys of silver and gold were suspended from his waist. After paying his respects he took his seat by me. The old lady said, "Baharvar, relate to this fakir whatever you saw in Neemroz." Baharvar said: "My friend, our princess has thousands of slaves. They are all engaged in trade. I am also one of those humble ones. She sends them to every country with merchandise worth thousands of rupees. When they return, the princess inquires of them the manners and customs of the countries they visit. Once I happened to go to the city of Neemroz. There I saw that all the people were clad in black and sighed all the time. It seemed as if a great calamity had befallen them. Whosoever I asked the reason thereof would not reply. I stayed there for many days and just wondered at this. One morning all the citizens, high and low, young and old, rich and poor assembled outside the city. The king of the country, mounted on his horse and accompanied by the nobles of his court, was also present there. They all stood in a long line. I also joined them to see what was to happen, for it seemed that they were waiting for someone to come. After an hour or so there appeared from afar a handsome young man about sixteen years of age. Riding a bull, he was foaming at the mouth and bellowing and had something in his hand. When he came nearer, he got down from the bull and gave what he had in his hand to the handsome attendant who accompanied him, then sat down on the ground holding the halter of the bull in one hand and a naked sword in the other. Taking the object from him, the attendant showed it to all from one end of the line to the other. Everyone wept and cried when they saw the object. After thus showing it to all and making them weep and cry, he returned to his master. As the attendant reached him the young man got up and with the sword severed his head from his body. He then mounted his bull and rode back the same way he had come. All those present there did not move and kept their place. After he had gone far away and out of sight, they returned to the city. I anxiously asked everyone to explain to me what I had seen. I humbly begged of them and even offered them money to solve the mystery of the young man for me but nobody explained, nor could I make anything of it. When I returned here I related to the princess what I had seen. She has been wondering ever since. She is extremely anxious to know what it all meant and decided that whoever gets for her the true explanation of this mystery, she will accept him in marriage and he will become the master of her wealth, country and herself.

'"You have now heard all about the strange event. Make up your mind. If you can bring any information about the young man you should set out for Neemroz at once; otherwise, don't accept the condition and go back to your country." I said, "If God wills it so, I shall find out all about it and soon return to the princess and fulfil my heart's desire. And if I am unlucky, I am helpless. But the princess should give me a solemn pledge that she will not go against what she has laid down as her condition for marriage, for this thought disturbs me. If she will be kind enough to grant me an audience and sit down behind the screen in her apartment and listen to my request and favour me with her reply, I shall be amply satisfied. Only then may I do what is required of me." The old lady conveyed it to the princess. She appreciated this and ordered her to call me before her. A maid conducted me to the princess's apartment.

'The apartment was magnificent! Her lovely female friends and good-looking servants and slaves—Turks, Ethiopians and Uzbeks—stood in two rows, dressed in rich jewels and with their arms folded in respect, each keeping her distance. What shall I call it? Indra's court of gaiety or an assembly of fairies? I was stupefied; my heart palpitated and involuntarily I sighed. However, I composed myself. Looking at the people around me I took my steps with heavy feet. With every beauty I looked at, my heart missed a beat. A screen was suspended at one end of the apartment and a seat studded with precious stones was placed near it. There was also another seat of sandalwood. The female-servant asked me to sit on the seat studded with precious jewels. She sat on the other one and said to me, "Now you may say whatever you have to say."

'After praising the princess for her justice and generosity I said, "Ever since I entered your territory I saw at every stage of the journey grand buildings for travellers to stay in and dutiful officials to look after them. I spent three days at every place. Even on the fourth day, when I intended to leave, no one would like me to depart. Moreover, I was told that whatever costly furniture and goods and carpets and utensils and all* that was used to serve me was mine and that I might take them away with me or lock them up in a room under my seal so that I could take them whenever I returned or else dispose of them in any way I pleased. I did as they advised. But I wonder at the huge sums of money spent if this humble traveller has been so generously treated and if all the thousands of travellers who happen to pass through your land are treated in the same way. How is it managed? Even the proverbial treasure of *Korah* would not suffice. And to all appearances, keeping all other expenses aside, the revenue from your territories would hardly be sufficient to meet even the expenses of your kitchen. I shall be satisfied if the princess herself may please explain the mystery to me. I may then be able to set out for Neemroz and, once there, solve the mystery as related to me and come back here, if I am spared my life, to devote myself to the service of the princess and thus find my peace of mind."

'The princess said, "Listen, young man, if you really wish to know the source of my wealth, stay here another day. I will send for you in the evening and you shall know all about it." Thus assured, I returned to the place where I was staying and waited for the next evening. In the meantime, a eunuch followed by porters with covered trays on their heads came to me and said, "Please have your dinner. The princess has sent some dishes from her own table for you." The mere sight of all the rich food so satiated me that I could eat very little of it and the rest I sent back. The next day, when the sun set like a weary traveller who had journeyed all day and the moon appeared in her assembly hall with her bright attendants, the female-servant came to me and said, "Come, sir, the princess has sent for you."

'I followed her to the private apartments of the princess. There was so much light there that even *Shab-e-Qadr* could not

---

* Here the author lists 48 items.

match it. A big cushion inlaid with gold and silver was placed on the costly carpets with a jewelled pillow near it. Over it was a canopy with a fringe of pearls, resting on poles studded with jewels. Shrubs made of precious stones of various colours projected from beds of gold decorating the spacious cushion seat whose flowers and leaves resembled real ones. Fair maids stood on either side with arms folded in respect. Dancing girls and female singers were also in attendance with their instruments well tuned and ready to perform. I was bewildered by the magnificence of the sight. I said to the female servant who had brought me, "There is so much gaiety and splendour in the day and such a splendid show at night that the day may verily be called Eid and the night *Shab-e-Barat*. Even a king of the seven climes cannot afford a more magnificent display. Is it always so?" She replied, "Of course, it is. The splendour increases day by day. Wait here while I inform the princess of your arrival. She is in the other room." With these words she left and returned soon after and took me to the room where I could present myself before the princess. I was all the more stupefied as I entered that room. I could not even distinguish between the door and the wall because large mirrors set in jewelled frames were fixed all around. As each reflected the other, it seemed that the whole room was inlaid with jewels. The princess was sitting behind a suspended screen. The maid took her seat by the screen and asked me to take mine. At the princess's command she said, "Listen now, young man! The sultan of this country was a great king. One day he held a grand fete at which all of his seven daughters, superbly dressed, were present. He said to them, 'Suppose your father was not a king and you were born to a poor man, would anyone have called you princesses? You should be grateful to God to be so called. You derive your good fortune entirely from me.' Six of his daughters in unison said, 'Whatever Your Majesty says is true. Our fortune rests on your welfare alone.' But this princess, though the youngest of them, yet even at that age more sensible and intelligent than the others, kept silent and did not join in the reply her sisters made as she firmly believed that to utter such words amounts to blasphemy. The king looked angrily at her and said, 'Well, my dear, you said nothing. Why so?' The princess tied her hands with her scarf and said, 'If Your Majesty will pardon me and grant me my life, I may humbly submit what is in my heart.' The king said, 'Say whatever you will.' The princess said, 'You are a mighty king but you know truth is mightier. So without caring a thought for my life I humbly submit that no one can rub off whatever God the Almighty, the Maker of Destinies, has written in my fate. And it cannot be changed:

Gratefully reconcile yourself to them
Or protest in anger,
Whatever your lines of fate decree
Will come to be, as they are stronger!

The Great King of Kings, who made you a king, has made me a princess. No one can have a say in His doings. You are our sovereign head and most respectable and dear to us. Even the dust of your feet I may kiss with respect but everyone is ruled by his own destiny.' The King was full of rage at these words. They came as a blow to his heart. In a fury of rage he said, 'A little mouth and such big words! The only punishment for her is this: let all the jewels on her person be taken from her, and she be taken in a litter and left in the wilderness where there may be no trace of a human being. Then we shall see what is written in her fate.'

'"Thus, accordingly, the princess, who had been brought up with all the love and care in the world and who had never been out of her apartments in the palace, was carried in a litter by the porters and left in a desolate place where even a bird would not fly. The sudden change had a strange effect on her. Now she would compare her changed circumstances with her past and then she would thank God and pray to him: 'Thou art Supreme and Independent, O Lord! Thou hast done what Thou hast wished to do, and whatever Thou mayst will Thou shalt do. Unto my last I shall not be despondent of Thy mercy!' Such were the thoughts in her mind when she fell asleep. She avoke before dawn and asked for water to perform her ablution. But then she recalled what had happened the previous night and said to herself, 'Now I am not what I was.' So she performed her ablution with dust and said her morning prayers. O young man, it is heartrending to relate the condition of the princess at that time. Just imagine what her innocent heart must have felt. There she was, alone with her trust in God and reciting these verses to herself:

> When one has no teeth Thou givest milk;
> When Thou givest teeth dost Thou not give food?
> He who takes care of birds in the air
> And of animals in water and on land,
> He will take care of you as well!
> Why do you feel so sad, O fool?
> It'll do you no good!
> He provides for the wise and the fool,
> He will provide for you as well!

How true! One remembers God when all hopes decay, otherwise every one regards himself wiser than even Aesop and Avicenna. Now behold the strange ways of God. Three days passed in this way and the princess did not have even a grain of food. Her delicate rose-like frame became feeble like a thinning thorn and her skin which had glittered like pure gold became pale. Her tongue was parched with thirst and her eyes became wooden and sank in their sockets. She could breathe only with difficulty. But whilst there is life, there is hope. On the fourth day a holy man came there. His face was bright like that of *Khizr* and he had a caring heart. Seeing the princess in this condition he said to her, 'Listen, my daughter, though your father is a king yet it was so decreed by your fate. Take this man as your servant and think of God the Creator, night and day.' He laid before her dry crumbs of bread from his wallet which he had received as alms and went in search of water. He found a well but there was neither a bucket nor a rope to draw water from it. He made a cup of leaves from a tree and used the cord tied round his waist as a rope. He drew water from the well and offered it to the princess. Thus she regained her senses. The holy man wept for the helpless and lonely princess and comforted her. From that day onwards he went in the morning to the city to beg alms and brought to the princess whatever scraps and crumbs he got. A few days passed in this way. One day as the princess untied the fillet to dress her hair, a pearl dropped down from it to the ground. She gave it to the holy man to sell in the city. He sold it and brought her the money. The princess then desired a house to be built there for her. The holy man said, 'Let us first do the earthwork to lay the foundations. I shall bring water. 'The princess started digging. Hardly had she excavated a yard deep when a door was discovered there. She removed the earth around it. Through the door she entered a large room which was full of gold sovereigns and precious stones. She took for herself four or five handfuls of the gold sovereigns and closed the door. In the meantime the holy man had returned. The princess now desired him to bring good masons and workers so that a grand royal palace like that of *Kisra* and grander than that of *Nu'mān* might be built there. She also said, 'Let the city-walls be erected, and a fort, a garden, a water-tank and a caravanserai be built in there as soon as possible. But first of all let them draw out the plans and show them to me.' The holy man brought skilful and efficient workmen and the construction work started. Honest and responsible men were appointed on different jobs.

"News of this grand building activity soon reached the king, the father of the princess. It was a big surprise to him. He inquired of his men about the princess who was responsible for this but no one could give him a satisfactory answer. To convince the king of their ignorance they even swore with their hands on their ears. So the king sent one of his nobles to the princess with the message that he wished to visit those buildings and also know about her royal family and country.

"'The princess was very happy to receive this message and wrote to the king, 'May God keep you! I am very glad to know of your wish to visit this poor abode. In fact, it will be a great honour to me. Blessed is the place where you tread and the dwellers on whom your shadow falls! May they thus be honoured and exalted by your kindly glance! I, the humblest of your servants, request that tomorrow, being Thursday and an auspicious day, will be more auspicious than the New Year's Day to me if Your Majesty will please grace us by your visit just as the sun brightens the worthless particles. May I also humbly request you to partake of whatever this humble being has to serve? To a stranger like me, it will certainly be an act of Your Majesty's kindness. To say anything more will be to exceed the bounds of respect!' She also made some presents to the nobleman who had brought the king's message and saw him off.

'"The king read the letter and sent her his word that he would visit the next day. The princess ordered her servants to make preparations for the king's reception and the grand feast so that he might be pleased and that whosoever, high and low, might accompany him should feel well-attended and satisfied. (On her directions such varieties of food were prepared that if a Brahmin girl had tasted them, she would have sworn by them, although she never takes such food.)

'"In the evening the king, seated on his uncovered throne, arrived at the princess's palace. The princess with her ladies-in-waiting proceeded to receive him. As she saw the king she made the royal obeisance with such respectful manners that the king was all the more impressed. With respect she accompanied the king to the precious throne. She had prepared a platform of 1,25,000 coins of silver for the king. A hundred and one trays of jewels and gold sovereigns and woollen shawls, silks, and two elephants and ten Arabian horses with their caparisons studded with precious stones, were also presented to him. After that she stood in respect before him with folded arms. The king politely asked her, 'Which country are you the princess of? And how is it that you have come here?' The princess, after paying her obeisance humbly said, 'This humble slave is the same offender who was sent to this wilderness by Your Majesty in a fit of anger. All that Your Majesty sees here is the wonderful doing of God.' These words warmed the king's heart. He rose and hugged her and made her sit near his throne. But he still wondered at what he saw. He asked the queen and the other princesses to be sent for at once. They came and seeing the princess there they wept with joy and embraced her and thanked God. The princess presented so much gold and jewels to her mother and sisters that the riches of the whole world could not equal even a part of it. The king asked them to take their seats and they partook of what was laid on the table for them.

'"Thereafter the king often visited the princess as long as he lived. At times he took her with him to his palace. When he passed away, the princess got his kingdom as she was the most competent to rule.

'"So, dear young man, this is all. The wealth given by God never exhausts, provided the beneficiary remains of good intent; the more one spends of it, the more one gets. To doubt God's power and grace is forbidden in every religion."

'After relating all this the old lady said, "Now if you still wish to proceed to Neemroz to bring any explanation of the strange event that has been related to you, you should leave at once." I said, "I am leaving for the place at this very moment. God willing, I shall return soon."

'Thus I took my leave and with trust in God I set out for Neemroz.'

Tale of the Prince of Neemroz

'It took me one year to reach Neemroz. I faced many difficulties on the way. On reaching there I saw that all the citizens, rich or poor, were really clad in black as I had been told. After a few days when the new moon appeared and it was the first day of the month following, all the citizens, high and low, young and old, men and women, went out with their king and assembled on a vast plain. Away from my country and wealth, almost like a beggar, I also followed them, wondering about what was to come. In the meantime, a young man appeared from the woods. He was riding a bull and foaming at the mouth as he made a bellowing cry. I had reached there after a hard and perilous journey only to unravel the mystery but on seeing the young man I was so wonderstruck that I stood transfixed. It was only after the young man had performed his cruel deed and left and the citizens started going back to the city that I realized I had done nothing.

Thinking that I would have to wait for another month I blamed myself for it. Helpless then, I also came back with the others.

'I counted the days of that one month like the month of Ramzan (month of fasts). At last when the new moon appeared, I was happy as if it signified the festival of Eid. On the first of the lunar month, the king and the citizens again assembled at the same place. This time I was determined to learn all about the strange event, come what may. Suddenly the young man appeared, as before, mounted on a yellow bull. When he came near he got off the bull and sat down on the ground. In one hand he held a naked sword and in the other the bull's halter. He gave a vase to his attendant who showed it to everyone and carried it back to his master. Everyone wailed and wept to see the vase. The young man broke the vase and with one stroke severed the head of his attendant from his body. Then he mounted his bull and started back towards the woods. I followed him fast but the citizens seized me and said, "What are you doing? Why do you want to lose your life? If you cannot bear it there are other ways you can put an end to it." Earnestly I pleaded with them to let me go and I tried to get out of their hold but I could not. Three or four men held me firmly and took me back to the city.

'It was such a painful shock. I had to wait another month. On the first day of the next lunar month the citizens again assembled there. I got up early at prayer time and went to the woods much before the others and hid myself at a place by which the young man had to pass. I did not wish anybody to deter me from my appointed task this time. The young man appeared as usual and returned after he had gone through the whole exercise. I ran after him. Hearing the sound of my footsteps he turned round the halter of the bull making a loud noise and frowned at me with rage. He drew his sword and threatened to charge at me. I stooped down and with utmost respect stood before him with folded hands. He seemed to understand these respectful manners and said to me, "O you wretched fellow, you were on the point of death. Luckily you are saved. You have still some life to live, it seems. Get away and don't follow me." With these words he took out a jewelled dagger suspended from his waist and throwing it before me he said, "At the moment I have only this dagger with me to give you. Take it to the king and you will get whatever you want."

'I was so awed by his fearful looks that I could not even move from my place or utter a word. I choked in my throat and my feet became heavy. The young man raised an awful cry and set out again. I said to myself, "Come what may, to let him go like this will not be fair. I will never get such an opportunity again." Regardless of the consequences, I followed him. He turned towards me and threatened to kill me. I lowered my head and entreated him in the name of all that was sacred and said, "O you, who are the *Rustam* of the day, give me such a blow that will cut me clean in two; let not a fibre remain intact so that I may be relieved of this miserable life. I pardon you my blood." He said, "You, the devil be, why do you bring your blood on me by making me commit the crime? Get away. Is your life such a great burden to you?" I did not mind his words and kept on following him. He pretended not to take any notice.

'We had gone about three or four miles into the woods when I saw a building. The young man went up to its door and screamed once. The door opened. He entered and closed the door after him. I remained outside, wondering about it all. After a short while a servant came out and said, "Come now; you are called in. It seems the angel of death is hovering over your head. It is your bad luck, perhaps, that has brought you here." "It is my good fortune!" I said and went with him into the garden. He conducted me to the place where the young man was sitting. I lowered my head in respect to him and he gestured me to sit down which I did, but kept my distance. He was sitting on a low table and the tools of a goldsmith lay before him. He had just finished carving a branch of emeralds. When it was time for him to wind up his work, all the servants hid themselves in rooms. I also hid myself in a room. The young man locked all the rooms except mine and went to the corner of the garden and started beating the bull. The bull cried out in pain and I trembled with fear. But since I had taken so many risks to unravel the mystery and although I trembled with fear, I slowly opened the door of my room and hid myself behind a tree to see what was going on. The young man threw down the stick and after unlocking one of the rooms, entered it. In an instant he came out and fondly patted the bull's back and kissed its muzzle. He put some grass before it and came towards the place where I had hidden myself. I quickly ran off into the room. The young man unlocked the rooms and all the servants came out. Some of them brought him water. He performed his ablution and after saying his prayers asked, "Where is that stranger?" No sooner had he said this, than I ran out and stood before him. He gestured me to sit down. Still keeping my distance, I took my seat.

Meanwhile the table was laid. He took his meal and also made me share it with him. After the dishes had been removed and we had washed our hands, he asked the servants to leave and take rest. When we were left alone he said to me, "Tell me, my friend, what calamity has befallen you that you are seeking your death?" I related to him the events of my life and said, "I look to your kindness alone to fulfil my wish." He heaved a sigh and in a thoughtless mood exclaimed, "O God, Thou alone knowest the pangs of love! One who has not known even a thorn-prick, how can he know the agony of others! He alone can fathom the pain of love who has felt it:

> *Let the tortures of love a lover tell,*
> *Not a feigner, but a lover indeed!"*

He tried to pull himself together but again a sigh issued from his heart, and the house echoed with it. I became convinced that he too was afflicted with love and that his malady was the same as mine. Taking courage I said, "I have told you all about my life; now do me a favour and kindly let me know about the events of your life. I will then first try to help you as much as I can in getting your heart's desire fulfilled." Accepting me as an intimate friend suffering from the same malady he said, "Listen, my friend! My heart is afflicted with this pain. I am the prince of Neemroz. The king, my father, called all the astrologers together at my birth and ordered them to cast my horoscope and ascertain the future course of my life. All of them after consulting each other said, 'By the grace of God, the prince is born under such an auspicious zodiac sign and at such an hour that he ought to rank as great as Alexander in the extent of his dominion and be equal to Naushervan in justice. He will be proficient in all the sciences and crafts and in whatever other branches of knowledge that might interest him. He will make such a name for himself by his charity and bravery that people will forget even Hatim and Rustam before him. But until he is fourteen he is exposed to great danger if he happens to see the sun or the moon. In fact, chances are that if he sees them he may go mad, recklessly shed people's blood and, becoming a cynic, take to the woods to live among birds and beasts. Guard him well; he shouldn't see the sun or the moon or even look towards the sky. If he is so guarded during the first fourteen years he will reign in peace and prosperity for the rest of his life.'

'"On hearing this the king ordered a garden to be laid out and got many apartments built in it. He ordered that I should be brought up in a vault with a dome lined with felt so that the light of the sun or the moon might not come in. With my wet-nurse and other female-servants I was brought up in that grand palace with the best care in the world. An experienced learned tutor was appointed to teach me the different sciences and crafts and all the styles of calligraphy. My father, the king, was keenly interested in me and kept himself informed of my progress every day. That very place was my world. I played with toys and flowers; and every delicacy was there for me to eat. I took whatever I wished. By the time I was ten, I had already made myself proficient in different branches of learning and craft.

'"One day an astonishing flower suddenly appeared high above in one of the ventilators of the vault. Even as I looked at it, it grew larger and larger. I tried to reach out for it but the more I stretched my hand towards it, the further away it moved. I was all the more surprised. As I kept my eyes fixed on it, I heard a loud laugh. Looking in that direction I discovered that the felt ceiling was broken in one place and a face as bright as the full moon appeared through it. I nearly fainted seeing it. However, I managed to stay on my feet and looked up again. To my astonishment I saw a throne studded with jewels raised on the shoulders of fairies. A fairy, elegantly dressed in shiny clothes and with a jewelled crown on her head, was sitting on it. She sipped some wine from the emerald-studded cup she held in her hand. Very slowly the throne descended and rested on the floor. The fairy beckoned me to sit by her side on the throne. She talked to me endearingly. Pressing her lips to mine and making me also drink a cup of that rosy wine she said, 'Man is unfaithful, I know, yet my heart is set on you.' She was so endearing. I was lost in her charms. It was as if I had tasted all the joys of life in that instant and felt that I had not lived till then.

'"But listen now to what followed and how our joys were marred. Carefree as we sat enjoying ourselves, four fairies descended from the heavens and said something in my beloved's ear. On hearing it she turned pale and said to me, 'My dear, I wish I could remain here with you for some time more and come here again and again or else take you with me, but the revolution of heavens does not let two persons remain together in peace. So farewell, my dear. May God keep you!' These words disturbed me much and I lost my senses. I cried, 'When shall we meet again? What do these dreadful words mean? Return soon if you wish to see me alive, otherwise you will regret it. Or else tell me your name and place so that I may be able to meet you.' She said, 'God forbid, may you live a hundred and twenty years! If we live, we shall meet again. I am the daughter of the king of the djinn and live on the Mountain *Qāf* at the end of the world.' The fairies then lifted the throne and it vanished into the sky as mysteriously as it had come down. As long as it remained in sight our eyes were fixed on each other. When it was out of sight I was completely lost. It seemed as if I was possessed of some evil spirit. Sadness sat heavy on my heart and the world appeared all dark to me. Distressed and confounded, I wept bitterly and threw dust over my head and tore my clothes. I lost interest even in food and drink, and became indifferent to everything, good or bad:

> *What strange afflictions this love may cause;*
> *It makes the heart restless and sad!*

My nurse and tutor knew my condition. Trembling with fear

they went to the king and said, 'Such is, unfortunately, the condition of the prince. We simply do not know how this calamity has befallen him. He has even lost his sleep and appetite.' The king immediately came to the garden-palace. He was accompanied by the vizier, nobles of the court, experienced physicians, learned astrologers and wise and holy men. He was distressed to see me restless and crying. He wept and with affection clasped me to his breast and gave orders for my treatment. The physicians prescribed medicines to soothe my nerves and strengthen my heart. The holy men wrote charms and amulets to be taken and worn by me. They also tried to exorcise the evil spirits. The astrologers suggested that alms be given since the misfortune according to them was brought by the revolution of the stars and the planets. In short, every one advised according to his profession. But I alone knew how I felt. No one's effort and advice was of any avail. My madness increased day by day and my body weakened for want of nourishment. I cried and moaned night and day.

'"Three years passed in this way. In the fourth year a merchant who had travelled far and wide came to my father's court. He brought my father many a present from different countries. He was well received and my father favoured him with an audience. After the formal greetings my father said, 'You have been to many lands. Have you ever come across a truly learned physician? Or have you heard of one?' The merchant said, 'Sir, I have been to many countries but the best physician I know of is a long-haired *gusā'īn*. He lives in a Mahadev temple built on a rock in the middle of a river in Hindustan. He has a fine house there in a lovely garden. Once a year, on the festival of Shivratri to be precise, he comes out of his house and takes a swim in the river. On his way back he examines the urine and feels the pulse of each of the sick and afflicted persons who come from far and wide and assemble at his door. He prescribes medicines and retires to his place. He is in fact the Plato of this age. God has given him such healing powers that his prescriptions prove to be highly efficacious and all kinds of afflictions are cured in no time. I have myself witnessed all this and praised God who has created such men. The prince may be taken to him for consultation if

Your Majesty be pleased. I am sure that the prince will be completely cured by him. The change of climate too will certainly do him good.' My father, the king, was pleased to agree with the merchant and said, 'Well, maybe my son gets well at his hands and his lunacy is cured.' He then appointed an experienced and distinguished nobleman of his court to accompany me. Arrangements were made for everything that might be needed. Many boats, large and small, were provided.* And so we embarked on them and he saw us off.

'"Travelling stage by stage we arrived at the place of the jogi. The change of climate had a soothing effect on my nerves. But still there was no break in my silence nor in my tears. The thought of the fairy still remained fresh in my mind. If ever I uttered any words they were these:

> *What a fairy I set my eyes on I do not know;*
> *But my heart was well-composed a little while ago!*

About four thousand sick people assembled on the rock during the two or three months since we reached there. Everyone of them believed that, God willing, the *gusā'īn* would completely cure all of them when he came out of his hut. On the appointed day the jogi appeared in the morning like the sun. He bathed in the river, swam across and came back. He rubbed ash over his body and thus made his fair form appear like burning coal in the ashes. On his forehead he made a mark with sandalwood powder. He tucked his dhoti between his legs and placed his angochha on his shoulders. He then tied his long hair in a knot, and put on his sandals. From his looks it appeared that the whole world meant little to him. He took his inkstand, studded with precious stones, and paper under his arm and after examining each and everyone prescribed medicines. Then he came to me. When our eyes met he stood still, paused for a moment and then said, 'Come along with me.' I followed him. He led me into a garden and asked me to reside there in a neat private apartment. Then he retired to his place. After

---

* The author lists eight kinds of vessels.

forty days he came to me and was pleased to find me better. He advised me to amuse myself in the garden and gave me a china pot full of medicine to be taken half a spoonful daily before breakfast. Then he departed. I acted upon his advice. I felt I gained strength of body and peace of mind. But the pangs of love remained as acute as before, for the fairy's lovely form always remained before my eyes.

'"One day I found a book on a niche. I took it down and as I read it I knew that it contained information about all that related to the world and religion. It was like an ocean of knowledge gathered in a small vessel. I read it every day and became quite adept in the science of physic and the mystic art of calling the spirits at my command. A year passed in this way and the appointed day of joy came again. The jogi came out of his house. I paid him my respects. Handing over his inkstand to me he asked me to accompany him. I followed him. When he walked out of the gate the huge crowd of people who had assembled there prayed for his long life. Seeing me with the *gusā'īn*, the nobleman and the merchant who had taken me there fell at his feet. They thanked him and said, 'It is by your kindness and care that the prince has made such an improvement.' He went to the river, bathed in it and said his prayers as usual. On his way back, he examined the sick and afflicted. Among the lunatics there was a handsome young man who could hardly stand because of weakness. He asked me to take the young man with me. After prescribing medicines for all he took us to his private room. There he opened the young man's skull a little. He was just about to seize with his pincers the centipede which had firmly clung to his brain when I at once said, 'Better if you hold it with a pair of hot pincers. Then it will uncling itself. Otherwise it will not release its grip and that can be fatal.'

'"The jogi looked at me and stood up. Without uttering a word he went to a corner of the garden, made a noose of his long hair round his neck and hanged himself. I reached him only to find him dead. I felt sorry for him but the only thing I could do was to bury his dead body. As I took it down from the tree, two keys dropped down from his hair. I picked them up and then laid that holy treasure of excellence under the earth. I tried the keys in all the locks of the rooms one by one and succeeded in opening two of them. They were both filled with jewels and precious stones. A locked chest, covered in velvet with gold plates fixed on it, was kept in a corner. I opened the chest and found a book therein which had the Great Name of God and the different modes of worship and prayers to call the djinn, fairies and the spirits and to control the sun. I was only too glad to find such a great treasure and started learning things from the book. I opened the garden gate and asked the nobleman and others who had accompanied me to put those jewels and books on the boats. Then we set sail for home. As we approached our country, the king, my father, learning of our arrival came to receive us riding on his horse. With affection he embraced me. I kissed his feet and said, 'May this humble being be allowed to live in the same garden-palace?' He said, 'Look here, my son, I think that the place has been inauspicious and I have forbidden them to keep it in good shape. So it is in no condition for you to live in. Live anywhere you please, preferably in the fort itself and within my sight. A garden may be laid out there for you as you please.' I was, however, bent upon having the same garden for my residence. I, therefore, got it renewed and well-adorned like the Garden of Eden, and started living there.

'"There I practised the spell which could enable me to call the djinn at my command. For forty days I abstained from meat and said my prayers to call the spirits. When the forty days were over, there came a terrible duststorm at midnight. Many huge buildings collapsed and mighty trees were uprooted. Then an army of fairies appeared and a throne descended from the sky. A person, richly attired and with a jewelled crown on his head, was sitting on it. I paid my respects to him. He returned my salutations and said, 'Why give me trouble, my friend? What do you want from me?' I humbly said, 'This humble being has been in love with your daughter for long. For her I have suffered much and wandered about in pain. Though alive I feel dead without her. I know I have done this at the risk of my life but I am desperate. All my hopes rest on you. Kindly consider my humble request and do me the favour of letting me see her. Thus you shall give me my life anew and it will be an act of real charity.

'"Thus informed of my heart's desire, he said, 'Man is made of earth and we are made of fire. It is difficult for the two to remain together.' I assured him that I only desired to see her and that I had no other wish. From his throne he said, 'Man does not keep his word. He may make a promise in time of need but he forgets it soon. Whatever I say is for your good alone. Remember, if ever you intend to do anything else both of you will be ruined. You may even lose your life.' I again swore to him and said, 'I shall not do anything which may bring us ruin. I only wish to see her.' We were talking to each other when all of a sudden the fairy we were talking about appeared. She was perfectly adorned. The throne of the king of fairies disappeared. I was beside myself with joy and with all fondness I embraced her and recited this verse:

> *Why shouldn't my mistress come to me*
> *With her eyebrows, each like a bow?*
> *I prepared for it for long*
> *And made a vow!*

We lived together in that garden and enjoyed ourselves. With her in my embrace I would only enjoy her outward charm, for I dreaded to think of any other joy. Finding me true to my word the fairy was surprised and at times she would say, 'You are so true to your word, my dear, but take one friendly piece of advice from me. You should always take care of your book lest the djinn should take it one day.' I said, 'I hold it dear to me as my life and guard it as I should.'

'"But one day as Satan would decoy me, in my passion for her I thought, 'How long, after all, shall I restrain myself? Come what may, I must have her!' I clasped her to my breast and intended to indulge with her. That very moment I heard a sound that said, 'Give me the book for it contains the Great Name of God. Do not desecrate it.' In that moment of passion I had no other consideration. I took the book and gave it, little realizing whom I was giving it to, and then I recklessly aimed to indulge with her. Realizing my foolish act the fairy said, 'Alas, you did commit the mistake and forgot my advice.' This much she had said when she fainted and I saw a djinn standing by her bed, holding the book in his hand. I wanted to get hold of him and take back the book after severely beating him when another djinn appeared and taking the book from him, ran off. I started reciting all the charms and incantations I had learnt, with the result that the djinn standing nearby turned into a bull. But alas, the fairy still did not regain her consciousness. She lay there as senseless as before and then disappeared. I was so disturbed. All my joys turned into bitterness. I lost all interest in the company of men from that very day and confined myself to this garden. Just to amuse myself I make a vase of emerald branches and mounting on that bull I go every month to the place where you saw me. There I break the vase into pieces and kill a slave. I do this all so that the people there may take pity on me and some pious man may one day pray to God and I get what I wish in my heart. This is all about my madness and lunacy, my friend."

'I wept on hearing his story and said, "You have really suffered too much in love, O prince! But I swear by God that I hereby give up my personal ambitions. Henceforth I shall wander about in woods and on mountains and do whatever I can for you." After giving my word I took my leave. For five years I wandered about from place to place but did not find any trace of the fairy. At last in my disappointment I climbed a mountain to hurl myself down into the valley. But a veiled horseman appeared and said mysteriously, "Don't waste your life; in a few days you are destined to fulfil your heart's desire."

'O holy men of God, I have at last joined you here and now I hope that by the grace of God happy days are ahead and all those who are despondent will get what they wish.'

When the second dervish finished the story of his life the night had passed and it was nearly dawn. Azad Bakht, the king, still unseen by the dervishes, returned to his palace. After having his bath and saying his prayers he dressed himself in the royal dress and sat on his throne in the Hall of Public Audience. He ordered a guard to go to the place of the four dervishes and bring them along. When the guard reached there he saw that the dervishes were ready to take leave of each other for the day after washing themselves. He said to them, 'The king has called you all in his presence. Please come with me.' The four dervishes looked at each other and said to the guard, 'We are masters of our will! What have we to do with the kings of the world?' The guard said, 'Holy Sirs, what does it matter? Please, come with me.' The four dervishes then recollected what Murtaza (Ali), the veiled rider who had prevented the first and the second dervish from committing suicide, had promised them. They realized that the time had come when their troubles would end, as had been foretold. So gladly they went along with the guard.

When they reached the fort and appeared before the king they blessed him saying, 'May you prosper ever more!' The king then went to the Hall of Private Audience and sent for a few chief nobles of his court. He also asked for the dervishes to be conducted there. When they were ushered in, he politely asked them to take their seats and said, 'Where do you hail from? And where do you want to go?' They replied, 'May you have a long life and prosper ever more. We are fakirs and have been wandering for long, and as it is said that a fakir's home is where the evening overtakes him, how can we relate what we have seen in this transitory world?' Azad Bakht comforted them and got the table laid. After breakfast he said, 'Please relate to me how you have fared in your lives. I shall do for you whatever I can.' The dervishes replied, 'We are sorry, for we have not the strength to relate what has happened to us; nor will the king be pleased to hear it.' The king smiled and said, 'I was present at the place where you were relating your adventures last night. So I have heard the adventures of two of you. Now I wish the other two also to relate theirs. Have no worry now, for as it is said, "the presence of dervishes wards off evil"; please stay here with me for a few days.'

The dervishes hesitated and sat there in silence. They did not have the power to speak before him. When Azad Bakht saw that they could not speak as they were perhaps overawed, he said, 'There is no one in this world who has not met with strange happenings in his life. I am a king, yet a strange event has also happened to me. First let me relate it to you. Kindly listen to it.' The dervishes said, 'Your Majesty, you are all kindness to us. Be good enough to relate it.'

The Tale of Azad Bakht

Azad Bakht, said:

'O holy men, you are masters of your will;
Please hear the adventures of a king;
Hear now whatever I saw or heard;
To you I relate it all!
Your attention, please!

'When my father passed away and I ascended the throne I was
in the prime of my life and the whole of Turkey was under
my dominion. One day a merchant from Badakhshan arrived
in my capital. He had with him a lot of merchandise. I was
told that such a big merchant had never visited the capital
before. I sent for him. He presented me many rarities from
different lands. Every present was costly, indeed. One of them
was a ruby in a little box. It had a fine shape and colour and
was just a little less then an ounce in weight. I had never seen
or heard of such a ruby before. I liked it and amply rewarded
the merchant for it. I granted him permission to travel freely
in my kingdom and allowed his goods to be transported duty
free. I also issued orders to accord him due hospitality and
protection and to indemnify his damage or loss. The merchant
regularly attended my court. He was well-versed in the manners
of the royal court and charming in his conversation. Every
morning I sent for the ruby from the royal jewel-store and
amused myself looking at it.

'One day I was holding court in the Hall of Public Audience.
The nobles and high officials took their seats according to their

ranks. The ambassadors and personal emissaries of many kings who had come to felicitate me on my accession to the throne were also present. I sent for the ruby, as was my practice, and the officer of the royal jewel-store brought it. With a word of praise I gave it to the Ambassador of Farang to appreciate its beauty. With a smile he praised it by way of flattery. It is was passed on from hand to hand and all of them said, "It is sheer good luck that such a ruby has come into Your Majesty's possession. No other king has ever possessed such a precious stone." My father's vizier, who was a man of wisdom and held the same position under me, was also present. With respect he said, "May I say a few words if I am granted my life?" I granted him permission to speak. He said, "Your Majesty, you are a mighty king and it does not befit a king to lavish so much praise on a mere piece of stone. No doubt, it is unique in shape and colour and weight, yet it is only a piece of stone. The ambassadors of different countries are present here. When they return to their countries they will certainly relate it to others and say: 'What a strange king he is who has got a ruby from somewhere and makes so much of it and shows it to everyone in his court.' Just imagine, how every king and rajah will laugh at you! Your Majesty, there is a merchant in Nishapur who has twelve such rubies, each more than an ounce in weight, and yet he has sewn them on to a dog's collar and the cur is adorned with them."

'I felt much offended at this remark and said in anger, "Let this vizier be put to death!" Immediately the executioners held him and as they were dragging him off for execution, the ambassador of the king of Farang came forward and stood before me with folded arms. I asked him, "What do you want?" He submitted, "May I know the vizier's fault?" I said, "What greater fault can there be than to lie and that too before kings?" He replied, "But Your Majesty, it is not yet proved that he has told a lie. Maybe what he says is true. It is not just to kill an innocent person like him." I said, "But it is unbelievable. A merchant takes great pains to earn profit, wandering about from place to place and saving every penny he earns. He will not waste precious gems on a dog's collar." He said, "Nothing is surprising before the power of God; what the vizier has said may be true. Indeed, merchants and holy men of God, more than anyone else, may come across such rarities, for they travel far and wide and collect whatever they think worth collecting. It will be more advisable to put the vizier in prison if he is guilty of being a liar as you think him to be. Viziers are the advisers of kings and it does not behove a king to get a vizier executed even before it is ascertained that he has told a lie and to forget all about his long loyal service. Your Majesty will be pleased to remember that former kings made prisons for this very reason. If a king is offended by someone he may imprison the person. It is possible that after his anger subsides he may relent or that the innocence of the person is proved. Thus the king will save himself from the guilt of shedding innocent blood and will not have to answer for it on the Day of Judgment."

'Much as I tried to justify myself, he argued against me so well that I could not win. So I said, "Well, I accept what you say. I grant him his life but he will remain in prison. He shall be released if the truth of his story is proved within a year's time, otherwise he shall be put to death." I then ordered him to be put in prison. The ambassador respectfully bowed and took his seat.

'When this sad news reached the vizier's family, they all cried with grief. He had a fifteen-year-old daughter who was beautiful, intelligent and well-educated. The vizier was extremely fond of her. He had built her an elegant apartment near his own drawing room. She had the daughters of the nobles as her companions and fair female-servants were kept in attendance for her. The day the vizier was put to prison, she was celebrating the marriage of her doll and they were preparing for the festivities at night. She was making sweetmeats for the occasion when her mother, her hair dishevelled, ran into her apartment barefoot. She wept and cried and broke the sad news to her. She reproached her and said, "I would have been better pleased if God had blessed me with a blind son instead of you, for he would have stood by his father." The daughter said, "What you think a blind son could do, I can do as well." Her mother said, "Let your face be smeared with dust! Your father is in great trouble. The king has put him in prison because he said something which displeased him." She said,

"Let me know what it is." Her mother replied, "Your father said that there is a merchant in Nishapur who has sewn twelve big rubies on his dog's collar. The king did not believe it. He took him to be a liar and so put him in prison. If we had a son he would not have remained idle until he got his father freed." The daughter said, "My dear mother, one cannot fight one's fate. Man should be firm and steady in the face of a sudden calamity and have trust in God. He is most compassionate and never keeps one in trouble. It is not proper to weep and cry, lest our enemies should incite the king against us. We should instead pray for the king always, for we are his servants and he is our master. He is displeased with us at this moment; he will be kind too." Thus the girl comforted her mother who then quietly left for her apartment.

'At night the vizier's daughter sent for her nurse's husband. She fell at his feet and wept and said, "I want to get my father released and thus wipe off the insult my mother has cast on me. If you could accompany me to Nishapur I may find the merchant who has rubies on his dog's collar, and do whatever I can to get my father released." At first he was reluctant but she implored him much till he agreed. She said to him, "Make secret preparations for the journey. Buy some goods for trade and presents good enough for kings. Also have some slaves and servants but be careful that no one comes to know of my plan." He carried out her orders and when everything was ready and the camels and mules were loaded, he set out. The vizier's daughter joined him disguised as a man. The secret was well kept and the people in the house learnt of the disappearance only the next morning. Her mother was afraid of the censure and reproof of people and hence did not disclose the circumstance of her disappearance.

'The vizier's daughter now called herself the son of a merchant. Taking rest at several stops on their way they reached Nishapur. They stayed at the caravanserai with their merchandise. In the morning, after having her bath and putting on a rich dress as the men of Turkey did, the vizier's daughter went out to have a stroll in the city. As she stood at a crossing in the main bazaar, she saw a jeweller's shop. Many precious stones were displayed there for sale, and richly dressed servants stood ready to attend. A man of about fifty years of age, who was elegantly dressed and appeared to be their master, was sitting there and talking to his companions who were also richly dressed like him. It occurred to her that he might be the merchant her father had spoken of to the king. She was pleased to think so and said to herself, "Would that my presumption is right! O my God, if only I could know more about this man!" As she looked around she saw two men in iron cages suspended in an adjacent shop. Both the men were pining away like the legendary Majnun; only their skin and bones remained. Their hair and nails were quite overgrown and they sat with their heads drooping to their breasts. Two ugly armed negroes stood as guards on either side of the two cages. The vizier's daughter was surprised at this and exclaimed to herself, "God alone is the Rescuer!" When she looked around the street she saw another shop where a dog was sitting on a velvet cushion on on ivory stool. It was chained by a chain of gold and its collar was set with precious stones. Two young handsome servants tended the dog. One of them had a fly-flap of peacock feathers with a handle covered with jewels, and the other had an embroidered napkin to wipe the dog's mouth and feet. The vizier's daughter looked at the dog more carefully and found that its collar really did have twelve rubies as she had heard. She praised God and wondered how she could take the dog with its collar of rubies and show it to the king and get her father released.

'As she stood there thinking of some such plan, the people around wondered at her beauty. They gazed at her and said to each other, "We have never seen such a beauty in this city." When the Khwaja, the jeweller, saw the *young merchant* (the vizier's daughter), he sent his servant to invite *him* to his shop. The servant went up to *him*. He delivered his master's message and said, "Please, be kind enough to favour us with a visit. Our master wishes to welcome you." As she herself wished it, she agreed. When she came nearer and the Khwaja saw *him* properly, he felt as if the spear of love had pierced his heart. He stood up to welcome *him* and just kept standing there stupidly, completely enamoured of *his* beauty. The vizier's daughter knew at once that he was caught in her charms. They embraced each other. The Khwaja, as he took her to be a merchant's son, kissed her forehead and offered her a seat next to his. With great interest he asked his name, about his family and country and where he was going. She replied, "This humble one is from Turkey. Istanbul is my native place. My father is a merchant. Now that he has grown old, he cannot undertake long journeys. He has, therefore, sent me to gain experience in commerce and trade. I have never been out of my country before. As it is my first journey, I did not travel by ship. I came by road. I had heard so much of your good name in the whole of Persia and I wished to have the honour of meeting you. Now that by the grace of God I have the honour, I find your good qualities to be much more than what they say. May God bless you! I will now proceed on my journey." On hearing these last words the Khwaja almost lost his senses and said, "Please don't, don't give me such a bad news, my son. Stay with me for a few days. Pray tell me where is your baggage? Where are your goods and your servants?" The vizier's daughter said, "A traveller's lodge is a caravanserai. Leaving my goods there I came to you." The Khwaja said, "It isn't right that a person like you who has come to see me should stay in a serai. I am quite well-known in the city, as you know. Please send quickly for your luggage. Let me also see the merchandise you have brought. I will so manage that you get the maximum profit. You shall thus save yourself the trouble of travelling further. You will also do me a favour if you stay here with me for a few days more." The vizier's daughter demurred but the Khwaja would accept no excuse. He asked one of his servants to send some conveyance quickly to the caravanserai to bring the goods. The vizier's daughter also sent a negro servant of her own with him while she herself remained there with the Khwaja until evening.

'After business hours, when the shop was closed, the Khwaja left for his house. One of the servants took the dog under his arm; the other took its ivory stool and velvet cushion. The armed negro guards placed the two cages on the porters' heads and went with them. Hand in hand and talking to her the Khwaja took the vizier's daughter to his house. She found it was a palatial house like that of kings and nobles, with carpets spread on the banks of a canal and articles of entrainment arranged before the main seat. The dog's stool was placed there. The Khwaja got the vizier's daughter seated by him. He entertained her with wine. When both of them got slightly intoxicated, the Khwaja called for dinner. The table was laid and delectable delicacies were served. First of all some meat in a dish covered with a golden cloth was taken to the dog. A cloth woven with golden threads was spread for it. The dog descended from its stool and ate as much as it liked. It drank water from a golden bowl and went back to its stool. The servants wiped its mouth and feet with napkins and carried that dish and bowl to the two cages. Taking the keys from the Khwaja and unlocking the cages they took the two men out, beat them with sticks and made them eat and drink the leftovers of the dog. Then they locked them up again in the cages and gave the keys to the Khwaja.

'After all this, the Khwaja began to take his meals. The vizier's daughter, displeased as she was to see all that, did not touch any dish. However much the Khwaja pressed her, she refrained. He, therefore, asked *him*, "Well, what is it? Why do you refrain?" She said, "Frankly, all that I have seen here is quite disgusting. Man is the crown of creation and a dog the most impure creature. Which religion would allow forcing any man to eat the leftovers of a dog? They are already your prisoners. Isn't that enough? Otherwise, as men, you and they are equal. You are not a Muslim, I presume. I don't know what you are. You seem to be a dog-worshipper to me. As such it is disgusting for me to be at your table unless you satisfy my curiosity." The Khwaja said, "I know what you mean. The citizens too condemn me and call me a dog-worshipper. But curse be on the impious and the infidels." He then recited the Mohammadan creed aloud. Thus was the vizier's daughter satisfied and said, "Well, then, if you are a Muslim, why do you do all this and stand condemned in the eyes of others?" The Khwaja said, "Yes, they condemn me. I pay double taxes as a fine for it too. But I don't want anyone to know the real cause of all this. It is really so strange and sad a story that one will get nothing but grief and indignation on hearing it. You also kindly excuse me for I do not have the power to tell nor will you have the heart to endure it." The vizier's daughter said to herself, "Why bother to press him! I should mind my own business." To him she said, "Well, if it is so, do not tell it." Then she had her dinner with the Khwaja.

'Two months passed and the vizier's daughter so cleverly acted a merchant's son that no one could tell she was really a girl. The Khwaja's affection for *him* grew day by day. Not for a moment would he like *him* to be out of his sight. One day when they were having their drinks, the vizier's daughter suddenly broke into tears. The Khwaja comforted *him* and wiping off *his* tears asked why *he* wept so. She said, "Sir, how shall I tell it? It would have been better for me if I had not met you and you had not been so good and kind to me. I face two difficulties now. Neither do I want to leave you nor can I stay here any longer. I must now depart but I feel there is little hope of my life after I leave you." The Khwaja wept bitterly to hear these words. He controlled himself and said, "You are the light of my eyes! Are you so soon wearied of me that you are thinking of leaving me sad and afflicted? Please discard this idea and stay with me as long as I live. I shall not be able to live without you; know it that in your absence I shall die even before I am claimed by death. You know the climate of this place is so good and congenial to health. Better if through a trustworthy servant you send for your parents and all their property. I shall stand for it. When your parents are settled here you will carry on your business and be completely satisfied. I have been through the thick and thin of life and I have myself been to many countries; but I have grown old now and have no issue. I hold you dearer to me than a son. I hereby make you my heir and the master of all my property. Take charge of all my business affairs. Only give me a little to sustain my life as long as I live. When I die, bury me and have all my wealth." The vizier's daughter replied, "You have really been more than a father to me. Your love and affection have, in fact, made me forget my parents. But my father gave me a year's leave. If I take longer to return he might kill himself with grief. You know a father's approbation is dear to God. If he gets displeased with me and, God forbid, curses me, I will be deprived of the grace of God in this world and the next. Now it will be most kind of you to permit me to leave and carry out my father's command and thus fulfil my duties as a son. If I safely reach my country I shall always remember your kindness and feel grateful as long as I live. God is the Causer of causes; maybe I am so fortunate that I will come back to kiss your feet."

'In short, the vizier's daughter so artfully entreated the Khwaja that he had to agree. As he had become so fond of her he said, "Well, if you can't stay here any longer, I will accompany you. I hold you as dear to me as the soul of my life; What use is the body without the soul? If you are so determined, take me also with you." Thus he also made preparations for the journey. He ordered his servants to arrange quickly for conveyance. When the news of the Khwaja's departure spread, other merchants of the city also decided to set out with him. Khwaja, the dog-worshipper, took with him his many servants, all his jewellery and other property and pitched his tents outside the city and camped there in a grand way. Other merchants also joined him with their merchandise as a result of which it became quite a big camp. Ascertaining the auspicious hour they set out on their journey. The merchandise was loaded on thousands of camels and the jewellery and cash on mules. Five hundred armed Tartar, African and Turkish slaves, mounted on well-bred horses, went along as guards. The Khwaja and the vizier's daughter (still disguised as a young merchant) were in the rear. They were richly dressed and mounted on sedans. The dog was comfortably seated on a low velvet-cushioned table in a rich litter on the back of a camel. At every stage of the journey all the merchants came to the Khwaja and ate and drank with him. The Khwaja praised God for the happiness of being with the young merchant. And thus did they proceed.

'They reached Constantinople and camped outside the city. The vizier's daughter said to the Khwaja, "Sir, if you so please, grant me permission to go and see my parents and arrange for your stay." The Khwaja said, "I am here for your sake alone. You may go and see your parents and arrange for my stay near your own place. But please come soon." The vizier's daughter went to her house. All those in the vizier's palace were surprised to see a *young man* enter the house. The vizier's daughter ran up to her mother and threw herself at her feet. She wept and said, "It is your daughter, my dear mother." The vizier's wife began to reproach her and said, "You vile girl, you proved to be very artful. You disgraced yourself and brought a bad name to the family. We wept for you and comforted ourselves thinking you were dead. Now go away from my sight." The daughter threw the turban off her head and said, "My dear mother, I have not been to any improper place. Nor have I done anything wrong. Whatever I have done, I did to fulfil your wish and get my father released from prison. God be praised! Through His kindness and your good wishes I have accomplished my task and brought the merchant of Nishapur with me and also his dog which has those rubies in its collar. I have not lost the innocence you bestowed on me. I disguised myself as a man simply to make this journey. Only a day's work remains more after which I shall get my father released and come back to live here with you. If you grant me leave I may go for one day and then come back to you."

'When her mother was convinced that her daughter had done the job of a man and had preserved herself well, she humbly praised God the Almighty. She embraced her with joy and kissed her. She gave her leave to go and said, "Do now what you think best. I have now full confidence in you."

'The vizier's daughter again disguised herself as a man and left to meet Khwaja the dog-worshipper. The Khwaja, meanwhile, impatient to see her, had left the camp and was proceeding towards the city. As the vizier's daughter was coming to the Khwaja and he was going to meet *him*, they crossed each other. Seeing *him* the Khwaja exclaimed, "Where had you gone leaving this old man all by himself, my son?" She said, "With your permission I had gone to my house but the desire to be with you did not let me stay there. So I have come back to you." They then camped in a garden on the banks of the river near the city gate. The Khwaja and the vizier's daughter sat down together and ate and drank. In the afternoon while they were relaxing, a royal guard happened to pass that way. He was surprised to see the huge camp. Thinking that it was some foreign dignitary who had arrived, he stood there and amused himself. The Khwaja's attendants asked him who he was. He told them that he was the chief chasseur of the king. They informed the Khwaja about him. The Khwaja asked a negro servant to go and tell him they were travellers and to convey that if he so wished he might come and have some coffee and smoke a pipe with them. The chasseur was puzzled to learn the name of the merchant. The Khwaja's servant escorted him to the camp and he found it all quite magnificent there with so many slaves and attendants and guards. He bowed low to the Khwaja and the *young merchant*. He was all the more puzzled to see a dog so highly treated there. The Khwaja offered him a seat and some coffee after which the royal chasseur begged leave. The Khwaja gave him many presents and a few rolls of fine cloth and saw him off.

'When he attended my court the next day, the chasseur mentioned the Khwaja and the *young merchant*. When I asked him more about them he related to me all that he had seen. I was quite displeased to learn of the stately treatment given to a dog and the confinement of two men in cages. I decided that such a man deserved to be killed. I ordered some of my men to go there immediately, cut off his head and bring it to me. The same Ambassador of Farang happened to be present at the moment in the court. He smiled at my orders. I was all the more filled with anger and said, "You ill-mannered man, don't you know it is highly disrespectful to grin and show your teeth in the presence of a king. It is better to weep than to laugh without reason." With respect he said, "Your Majesty, many thoughts came to my mind and made me smile. The first was that the vizier had spoken the truth and now he will be released from prison. Second, Your Majesty has been saved from shedding innocent blood. Third, it occurred to me that Your Majesty ordered the merchant to be put to death without any fault. And it surprised me much that without finding out the truth or otherwise, Your Majesty should order to kill a person when someone only tells you a strange tale about him. God knows what the truth is about the merchant. Better call him here and ask him his true story. And then if he is found guilty he may be punished as Your Majesty may please."

'When the ambassador thus explained himself, I too was

reminded of what my vizier had said. So I ordered the merchant
to be produced before me with his son and his dog and the
cages with the two persons within. The guards immediately
left and brought them. I called them before me. First the Khwaja
and his son (the vizier's daughter) came forward. They were
richly dressed. All were astonished to see the beautiful *young
merchant* (the vizier's daughter) who laid before me a golden
tray full of jewels which illuminated the whole place. After
bowing down *he* stood in respect to me. The Khwaja also kissed
the ground and invoked blessings of God on me. Sweetly did
he speak like a singing nightingale! In my heart I admired his
eloquence and good manners but feigning anger I said to him,
"You are a devil in the garb of a man! What is this devilish net
you have cast? You have dug an infernal pit for yourself! What
is your religion and what rite is this? What prophet do you
follow? Even if you are an infidel, what is the idea behind all
this? What is your name and what exactly do you aim at?" He
said, "God bless Your Majesty and may you prosper ever more!
The religion of this humble being is this: God is One; He is
Incomparable; Muhammed (God bless and keep him and his
progeny!) is His messenger; after him I hold his four companions
and the twelve *Imams* as my guides; I say my prayers five times
a day and observe fasts and I have also performed my Haj
pilgrimage; I distribute one-fifth of my wealth as alms and
charity; and I am a Muslim. But there is a reason, which I
cannot disclose, for all that I do and for which I am condemned
by everyone and I have earned your displeasure too. They call
me a dog-worshipper and I have agreed to pay double taxes
for it but I have not disclosed my secret to anyone." I was all
the more enraged to hear these words and said, "You want to
fool me with all these excuses. I am not going to be carried
away by any one of them. You will not save your life unless
you give sufficient reasons for your wayward behaviour. Know
it that I will get your belly torn open as an exemplary punishment
so that no one may dare to defile the Muhammedan faith."
The Khwaja said, "Your Majesty, please do not shed the blood
of this ill-fated humble being. Confiscate all my boundless
wealth instead, and please spare my life and my *son's*." With
a smile I said, "So you want to bribe me with your wealth.

Know it, you fool, you will not be spared your life unless you tell the truth." The Khwaja burst into tears. He looked towards his son, raised a sigh and said to *him*, "I am a criminal in the eyes of His Majesty. What shall I do now? Who shall I entrust you to?" I threatened him and said, "You impostor, enough of these excuses! Stop all this and whatever you have to say, say it quickly!" He came near the throne and kissed it. He then praised me and said, "Your Majesty, if you had not ordered me to be put to death, I would have gladly undergone every pain and suffering rather than relate my story. But life is dear to everyone. No one likes to jump into a well. To save oneself is, therefore, right. And not to do what is right is against the commandment of God. If Your Majesty be so pleased, I humbly relate the story of my life. But first please let the two cages, in which the two men are confined, be brought before you. I now begin my life-story. Please confirm from them and convict me if I tell a lie and let justice prevail." I appreciated what he said and got the two men out of the cages and made them stand by his side.

Adventures of Khwaja the Dog-Worshipper

'The Khwaja began, "Your Majesty, these men are my brothers. The one on the right is the eldest. I am younger than both of them. Our father was a merchant in Persia. When I was fourteen he passed away. After the burial ceremonies and other rites were over, both these brothers said to me, 'Let us now divide our father's property and let each do with his share what he likes.' I said, 'My dear brothers, why do you utter such words? I am like your servant. I do not claim equal rights with you. Our father is dead but I take you both in his place. What I need is a little to sustain myself only to be able to remain in your service. What shall I do with my share? I will rather live on your charity and remain with you. I am just a boy and have not yet learnt to read and write. Look after me, please. This is all I want.' They said, 'So you want us also to be wronged and ruined with you!' Quietly I retired to a corner and wept. I said to myself, 'They are my elder brothers, after all. They show anger so that I may learn something and improve myself.' With these thoughts I fell asleep. In the morning a bailiff of the Qazi came and took me with him to his court. Both these brothers were already there. The Qazi asked me, 'Why don't you agree to divide your father's property?' I repeated to him what I had said to my brothers at home. They said to me, 'If you really mean what you say, let us have a release from you stating that you have no claim, whatsoever, on our father's property.' Even then I said to myself, 'As they are my elders, whatever they say will be for my good. Perhaps they apprehend that I might waste all my share.' So I gave them the release with the Qazi's seal. They were satisfied and we returned home.

'"The next day they said to me, 'O brother, dear, we require the apartment where you live. You better hire another place.' It was then that I realized they did not even want me to live in my father's house. I was helpless and so I decided to leave the house. Your Majesty, as everyone loves the youngest child most, my father used to give me some of the presents and rarities he brought with him from the different lands he visited. I sold those presents and raised a small capital of my own. With that sum I ran a small business. Once my father had brought a slave-girl for me from Turkey whom I kept. And once he gave me a colt which I used to feed out of my own pocket. I sold the colt and bought a house and shifted there. I bought some household goods and two slaves to serve me. With the remaining amount and with trust in God, I started running a cloth shop. I was contented with my lot. My brothers had been unkind but God was kind to me. Within three years I had established myself and was counted a man of credit. Every costly item required by nobles and officials could be had from my shop. I made a lot of money and lived in comfort and ease. I praised God and would often recite:

Let the king be displeased;
We have nothing to do with him.
Thou art the King of kings, O my Lord,
Thee alone I shall adore.
Let my brothers be displeased;

They can do me no harm.
Thou alone art the Rescuer;
Who else but Thee shall we look to for help!
Let the friend or foe be displeased,
Thou alone wilt carry me through.
The world is displeased with me
But Thou art above the world;
If Thou art not displeased with me
All the people will kiss my feet.

One Friday I was sitting at home when a slave of mine who had gone out to purchase some household goods returned with tearful eyes. I asked him the reason. Rather harshly he said, 'What is it to you? You live in comfort and enjoy yourself but how shall you explain all this on the Day of Judgement?' I said, 'You nigger, what calamity has befallen you?' He said, 'A Jew has got your brothers' hands tied behind their backs and he is belabouring them with a stick out there in the street. He is deriding them and says, "If you do not pay me my money I will beat you to death and it will be a good deed for me." This is how your brothers are being treated and you do not care. Just imagine what people will say?' Hearing this a fraternal feeling warmed up in me and asking my slaves to bring some money after me, I ran out barefoot into the street. There I found that the slave had not at all exaggerated. My brothers were indeed being cruelly beaten. I pleaded with the bailiffs not to beat them and to allow me to ask the Jew the reason for this cruel punishment. I went to the Jew and said, 'It is Sabbath today. Why are you beating them?' He said, 'If you really mean to plead for them, pay me my dues or mind your own business.' I asked, 'What money? Show me the deed and I'll settle it here and now.' He said he had filed the deed in the court. Meanwhile, my slaves brought me two bags of money. I gave a thousand pieces to the Jew and got my brothers released. They were hungry and had no clothes on their bodies. I took them to my house and gave them new clothes to wear and sent them to the bath. Then they had a hearty meal with me. I said nothing about their shares of our father's wealth lest they should feel ashamed. They are here; Your Majesty may please ask them if it is not true. A few days later when they recovered from the bruises and pain of the beating I said to them, 'My dear brothers, you have lost your credit in the city. Better if you go on a journey for a few days.' They agreed. I arranged for conveyance and tents and purchased merchandise worth twenty thousand for them. Then I sent them along with a caravan to Bokhara. After a year the caravan returned but I heard nothing about them. I asked a friend to tell me on oath what had become of my brothers. He said, 'When they reached Bokhara, one of them lost all his money at a gambling house and presently he is a sweeper there. He keeps the dice plank clean for gamblers and waits on them. He lives on what they give him as alms and charity. The other became enamoured of a brewer's daughter. He spent on her all he had and now serves at the brewer's shop. The people of the caravan do not relate it to you lest you should feel hurt.' I was so disturbed to hear all this that I could neither eat nor sleep. Taking some money with me I at once left for Bokhara. I found them with great difficulty and brought them to the place where I stayed. I asked them to bathe and got them new clothes. But I didn't say a word to them lest they should feel ashamed.

'"I again purchased goods for them and set out for home. When we reached a village near Nishapur I left them there with all the goods and came secretly to my house so that no one might know of my return. After two days I made it known that my brothers had returned from their journey and that I would go out to receive them the next day. In the morning, as I was about to leave, a man from the village came to me. He was crying. I asked him the reason. He said, 'Our houses have been plundered because of your brothers. Would that you had not left them there!' I said, 'But tell me what happened.' He said, 'A gang of robbers came at night and plundered their goods and ransacked our houses too.' I felt pity for them and asked where my brothers were. He replied, 'They are outside the city, distressed and with no clothes to wear. Immediately I took clothes for them and reached there, got them properly dressed and brought them with me to my house. Hearing of the robbery the neighbours came to see them. My brothers would not leave the house out of shame.

'"Three months passed in this way. I thought, 'How long will they remain confined? Better if I take them with me on a business trip.' I put this proposal before them. They kept silent. So I made preparations for the journey, purchased goods and set out with them. After I had distributed alms and loaded the goods on the boats, the anchor was weighed and we set sail. This dog was sleeping on the shore. When it saw the boat sailing away it barked, jumped into the waters and swam towards the boat. I sent a small boat for it and it was brought onto our vessel. We safely passed a month on the waters. During this period my second brother became enamoured of my slave-girl. He said to the eldest brother, 'It is shameful for us to remain under the obligation of a younger brother. How shall we pay for it?' The eldest confided to him, 'I have a plan. If we are able to carry it through, it will do.' So together they made a plot to kill me and thus take all my wealth and property.

'"One day when I was asleep in my cabin and the slave-girl was giving me a massage, my second brother came in and woke me up. He asked me to come with him. Startled, I followed him. This dog also followed me. I saw my eldest brother leaning over the side of the boat and closely watching the waters as he called me. I went up to him and said, 'What is it? All is well, I hope.' He said, 'Just look, look here. It is a strange sight. Mermen are dancing under the water with pearl oysters and branches of coral in their hands.' I would not have believed such a stupid thing had anyone else said it; since my elder brother said it, I took it to be true and leaned over to look. However much I tried I couldn't see any such thing. But he kept on saying, 'See! do you see it? Do you see it?' Had there really been any such thing, I would have seen it. When they found that I was not on my guard, my second brother gave me such a strong push from behind that I could not keep my balance and fell into the sea. They stood there crying, 'Come, help, our brother has fallen overboard.' The boat sailed forth and the waves carried me away from it. After a while I was completely exhausted and in my heart I prayed to God. Then my hand struck something. I looked at it. It was this very dog. When they pushed me overboard, it had also jumped into the waters and kept swimming next to me. I held on to its tail.

God made this dog the cause of my survival. Seven days and nights I passed in this manner. When at last on the eighth day we drifted to the shore, I had no strength left within me. I rolled and staggered along and somehow threw myself on dry land. For one whole day I lay completely unconscious. On the second day I heard the dog's bark as I came to myself. I praised God. Looking around I perceived a city far away, but where had I the strength to go there! I would crawl a bit and then rest. In this way I managed only about two miles by the evening. There was a hill on the way to the city. I lay there all night. The next morning I reached the city.

'"There in the city I saw shops of confectioners and bakers. How I wished to have something from them, but I had no money and I would not beg. I went along, saying to myself that I would ask for something at the next shop. At last whatever little strength I had gave way and my stomach burned with hunger. I was about to collapse when perchance I saw two young men dressed like Persians coming along arm in arm towards me. I was happy to see them and I thought of relating to them my sad plight if they were of my acquaintance. When they came near I discovered they were my own brothers. I was overjoyed and thanked God that He had spared me the disgrace of begging from others. I went up to them and greeted them and kissed the eldest brother's hand. Recognizing me they raised a hue and cry. The second brother slapped me in my face with such force that I staggered and fell to the ground. I held the eldest brother's robe and hoped he would help me. But he gave me a kick. In short, both of them beat me much and behaved with me as Yusuf's brothers had with him. However humbly I requested them to desist, for God's sake, they showed no pity. Meanwhile, people crowded there and asked them what my fault was. These brothers of mine said, 'This rascal was our brother's servant. He pushed him overboard and has taken all his property. We have been in search of him for long. Today we have found him here.' To me they said, 'You cruel being, what got into your head that you killed our brother? What wrong had he done to you? Was it so bad a thing that he made you incharge of his affairs?' They tore their clothes and wept and wailed feigning grief for their brother and beat me mercilessly. In the meantime the bailiffs of the magistrate arrived there. They rebuked them and said, 'Why do you beat him thus?' Then holding me by my hand they took me to the magistrate. These two also went along and repeated the same false story to him. They bribed him and sought blood for blood. The magistrate asked me if I had anything to say. I could not even utter a word in reply because I was already exhausted by hunger and the severe beating received at their hands. I stood silent, hanging my head down. Thus the magistrate concluded that I was indeed guilty. He decreed that I should be taken to an open piece of land and hanged on the gallows.

"'I had paid money to get these two released from the Jew's bondage, Your Majesty, but they spent money to take away my life in return. They are both present here. They may be asked if I have said anything but the truth in relating all these events. Well, I was taken to an open piece of land. When I saw the gallows I took myself as lost. Except this dog none else was there to grieve for me. Restless, it rolled on the ground and licked everyone's feet and barked. Some beat it with sticks and others threw stones but it would not leave that place. I stood with my face turned in the direction we face when we say our prayers and in my heart I prayed to God: 'In this moment of distress I have no one except Thee to help and save an innocent one like me. Only if Thou savest am I saved.' Then I recited the creed aloud and staggered to the ground.

"'Mysterious are the ways of God. It so happened that the king of that country suddenly developed a shooting colic pain. The nobles and the physicians assembled. No medicine proved effective. A holy man said, 'The best medicine will be to give alms and to release the prisoners. Prayer is better then medicine.' Immediately royal messengers ran towards the prison. One of them happened to pass our way too. Seeing the crowd he inquired and found that I was going to be hanged. He thus galloped fast towards the gallows and cut the ropes with his sword. He rebuked and threatened the magistrate's men and said, 'What is this? At a time when the king is in such agony you are putting a man, a creature of God, to death!' Thus he got me released. But these two brothers went to the magistrate

and again urged him to put me to death. As he had been bribed
he did what they told him to do. He said, 'Rest assured. This
time I'll put him in such a prison that he will starve to death
and nobody will even know of it.' So I was detained by him.
There was a mountain about two miles away from the city in
which a djinn had dug a dark, narrow well in the times of
Solomon. It was called the Prison of Solomon. Whoever earned
the wrath of the king was confined to that well and there he
met his death. In short, these two brothers and the magistrate's
men carried me there secretly at night. They returned satisfied
after pushing me into that well.

"Your Majesty, this dog had followed me to that well and
when they'd pushed me in, lay by its wall. I was unconscious
for quite a while. When I regained consciousness I thought I
was dead and that the place was my grave. I heard two men
talking to each other and I thought they were the two angels
who had come for my reckoning. When I felt about me I found
some bones in my hand. After a while I heard a sound as if
someone was eating something. I exclaimed, 'O creatures of
God, tell me for God's sake, who are you?' They laughed and
said, 'This is Solomon's Prison. We are prisoners here.' 'Am I
still alive?' I asked them. They laughed heartily and said, 'As
yet you are, but soon you shall die.' I said, 'What are you
eating? Give me also a little bit of it.' They got angry at this
and gave me only a coarse reply. After eating they fell asleep,
while I lay half-conscious, weeping and praying to God.

"'Your Majesty, for seven days I had been in the sea and
for so many days after that I had remained without food due
to my brothers' false accusation. I had been beaten too and
was now confined to a prison there was no way to come out
of. It was as if I was facing the agonies of death. Life seemed
to come and go. Sometimes a person came at midnight and
lowered the end of a rope with some bread tied in a piece of
cloth and a small earthen jar. The two men confined with me
would take it all for themselves. Out of pity for me this dog
tried to bring me food and water. It went to the city where
there were always loaves of fresh milk-bread piled up at the
bakers. Seizing one in its mouth, it ran off. People chased,
pelting it with stones, but it outran them; when the dogs of

the city attacked, it faught them all and saved the bread for me. When it dropped the bread into the well, it barked. In the daylight streaming in, I saw the loaf and grabbed it. The dog then went to find some water. Outside a hut in a village nearby, where an old woman was busy spinning at a wheel, it saw two earthen pots full of water. It tried dragging one away with its mouth but ended up breaking both the pots. Now when the woman charged at it with a stick, it rolled on the ground and began rubbing its muzzle on her feet and wagging its tail. Frantically it would run towards the mountain and then back to her, pulling her by the hem of her dress. By the grace of God, that kind woman guessed what the dumb animal wanted and followed it with a bucket of water which she lowered into the well. I drank a few draughts of water, ate what was left of the milk-bread and then retired to a corner to await what fate had in store for me. This ritual was repeated almost every day. Soon the bakers got used to the dog and, taking pity, would throw it a loaf whenever they saw it. And if some day the old woman failed to bring water, all her pots would be broken. Thus, this faithful animal kept me alive for six months—though, confined to such a prison and reduced to a skeleton with no fresh air reaching me, life had become a burden to me. I often wished I was dead.

'"One night when the two prisoners were asleep and my heart was heavy with grief, I broke into tears and humbly prayed to God. And lo, in the last quarter of the night I saw a rope dangling near me and heard a low voice saying, 'O unfortunate being, hold the end of the rope firmly in your hands and come out of the well.' I thought my brothers had had a change of heart and had come to take me out of the prison. I was overjoyed at this thought. I tied the end of the rope round my waist and was slowly pulled out. It was a dark night so I could not see the face of my benefactor. When I came out of the well, he said, 'Come, be quick. We should not stay here any longer.' Although I hadn't strength enough to walk down the mountain, my fear pushed me to the spot where two saddled horses were ready for us. The stranger helped me mount one of them. He mounted the other and led me to the' banks of a river. By morning we had journeyed twenty miles away from the city. I looked at the stranger. He was well-armed and was gazing angrily at me now. Obviously I was not the one he had come to rescue. Realizing his mistake he bit his finger and suddenly charged at me but I parried his thrust by falling from my horse. I appealed to him for mercy and said, 'I am innocent. Why do you want to kill me? You have been so kind. After rescuing me from such a horrid prison what will you get by killing me?' 'Tell me the whole truth about yourself,' he demanded. I said, 'I am a traveller but fell into this misery due to bad luck. It is by your kindness that I am still alive.' My entreaties made him pity me. He sheathed his sword and said, 'Well, God does what He wills. Get up now, I spare you. Mount your horse quickly. This is no place to stay.' We spurred our horses and went on. On the way he regretted and repented much. After midday we reached an island. There he got off his horse and made me also alight. He took the saddles off the horses and let them loose to graze. He also took off his arms, sat down on the ground and said to me, 'O you miserable wretched fellow, now let me know who you are.' I told him of my antecedents and all that had happened to me.

The Princess of Zerbad

'"When he heard my life-story he broke down and said, 'Now you listen to my story. I am actually the daughter of the king of Zerbad and the young man confined in Solomon's Prison is Bahramand, the son of my father's minister. One day the king ordered all the nobles and princes to assemble on the plain near the seraglio and exhibit their horsemanship and skill at polo and archery. I was seeing all this through a lattice from the upper storey of the palace with the queen, my mother, and nurses and friends. The minister's son was the most handsome of them all. He ringed and lounged his horse with great skill. I became enamoured of him. However, for quite some time I kept it a secret. When I grew too restless I confided in my nurse and gave her many presents so that she would help me. She somehow managed to bring that young man secretly to my apartment. He also fell in love with me. For many days we had our secret rendezvous till one night the guards caught hold of him when they saw him enter my room, and informed the king. Enraged, the king ordered him to be put to death. But as the high officers of State pleaded for him he was spared his life and sent to Solomon's Prison. The other young man imprisoned with him is his close friend. He was with Bahramand that night when he was caught. Both of them were put in prison and they have spent about three years there but even now nobody knows why they had come to the king's palace. God preserved my honour and out of gratitude to Him I took upon myself to provide the two prisoners with bread and water. Since then I have gone there every week with provisions for them. Last night I had a dream in which somebody said to me, "Get up quickly, take a horse and some clothes and money with you and go to the prison-well and rescue that unfortunate man." This dream woke me from my sleep. In fact, I rejoiced at it. I disguised myself as a man, filled a little box with jewels and gold sovereigns and taking a horse and some clothes with me, reached there to get him out of prison. But it was perhaps so destined that I should do this for you. No one knows what I have done. Perhaps it was some god who made me go there and get you released. Well now, I got what my fate held in store for me.'

'"After relating all this she took out some fried cakes of flour and pulse and cooked meat which she had in a piece of cloth. But first she dissolved some sugar in a cup of water, added some *musk* to it and gave it to me to drink. Then I had some breakfast. A little later, draping me round my waist she took me to the river and cut my hair and nails. After giving me a wash she dressed me and thus helped me look like a man again. I turned my face in the direction we say our prayers. The beautiful girl watched me perform my prayers. When I had finished she asked, 'What is it that you have done?' I said, 'I have offered my thanks to God the Almighty who has created the universe, who is Incomparable, who filled the heart of a beautiful one like you with kindness for me and sent you to rescue me from that horrible prison and attend to me.' She said, 'So you are a Muslim?' I replied, 'Thank God, I am!' She said, 'I am pleased with what you say. Teach me all these prayers.' I said to myself, 'Praise be to God, she is inclined to embrace our faith.' So I recited the creed to her and asked her to repeat it after me. Then we rode further on. When we halted at night she talked of our religion and faith and was pleased to hear what I said about it.

'"In this way we journeyed on for two months till we arrived in a country between Zerbad and Sarandip. We entered the city. It was more populous than Istanbul and its climate was excellent for health. The king of that country excelled even Cyrus in justice and in protection of his subjects. We were happy to be there. I bought a big house and a few days later, after getting over the fatigue, I purchased some household requirements, married the young lady according to the Muhammadan rites and settled there. Within the next three years I made contacts with the high and low of the city, started a business and established my goodwill. Very soon I surpassed all other merchants in business.

'"One day as I was going to wait on the Prime Minister I saw a huge crowd assembled in an open piece of land. On inquiring I gathered that two persons convicted for stealing and adultery, and perhaps for murder too, had been brought there to be stoned to death. This reminded me of a similar circumstance when I had been taken to the gallows but God had saved me then. I said to myself, 'I wonder who they are. Maybe they are falsely implicated like I was.' Making my way through the crowd I found that they were my brothers. Their hands were tied behind their backs and they were bareheaded and barefoot. I was grieved to see them in that condition. I gave the guards a handful of gold sovereigns and requesting them to wait, rode fast to the magistrate's house. I gave him a costly ruby as a present and pleaded for my brothers. He said, 'There is a plaint against them; their crimes have been proved; the king has already given his verdict. I am, therefore, helpless.' However, as I implored him much he sent for the complainant and made him agree to accept five thousand silver coins as blood-money which I paid and thus got them released. Your Majesty may please confirm it from them." The two men stood silently with their heads hanging in shame. "Well," the

Khwaja continued, "after getting them released I took them to my house, sent them to the bath and got them properly dressed. I provided for their stay with me in my drawing-room. This time I did not introduce them to my wife. I remained at their service, had my meals with them and retired to my apartment only at night.

'"For three years I thus served them. They also did not do anything to disturb me. When I went out they remained at home. One day it so happened that my wife, that virtuous woman, went to the bath. When she came to the drawing-room she took off her veil as she saw no one there. But perhaps this second brother of mine lay there and was awake. One look and he was enamoured of her. He confided in the eldest brother. Together they made a plot to kill me. I knew nothing about it. I rather thanked God in my heart thinking they had done nothing wrong this time and that they had finally mended their ways for fear or for shame.

'"One day after we had taken our meals, the eldest brother, with tearful eyes, spoke of the delights of Persia, our homeland. The other one also began to sigh. I said, 'If you so wish, let us go. I'll do as you please. I myself wish it. If God the Most High wills it so, I will also accompany you.'

'"I told my wife of my brothers' depression and also of my own intention. She wisely said, 'You know better, but I feel that they want to do some mischief again. They are your deadly enemies. You have taken snakes to your bosom and you trust them. You may do whatever you please but be on your guard against these wicked fellows."

'"Anyway, within a short time preparations were made for the journey. We pitched our tents on a plain. It became quite a big caravan and they made me their chief. We started at an auspicious hour. I remained on my guard against my brothers as best as I could, though I feigned to act on their advice to please them.

'"One day as we camped on our way, my second brother said, 'About four miles from here there is a spring, like that of the Garden of Eden, and for miles and miles together there bloom wild tulips, lilies, narcissus and roses. It is really a delightful place worth a visit. I would love to go there tomorrow if I could and enjoy the sight. Thus we could relieve ourselves of fatigue.' I said, 'You are certainly a master of your will. If you so wish we may stay there tomorrow and enjoy the sights.' So I let it be known in the caravan that we would stay there one day more. I asked the chief cook to get things ready for breakfast as we would leave early to enjoy the sights. At dawn, after changing their clothes, these two brothers of mine suggested we leave in the cool of the morning. I called for my horse but they said, 'You will enjoy the sights better if you go on foot rather then ride a horse. You may tell the grooms to lead the horses after us.' Two attendants carried the hooka and coffee pot while we amused ourselves by shooting arrows. When we had gone quite a distance from our camp they sent one attendant on some errand. After going a little further they sent the other attendant to call the first. As luck would have it, I remained silent as if my lips were sealed. They did what they wished and to divert my attention they kept me engaged in conversation. However, my faithful dog remained with me.

"'We had gone quite far away from our camp but I did not see any spring or flowers there. It was just a thorny wilderness. While I sat relieving myself there I perceived behind me the flash of a sword. As I turned to see, my second brother charged at me with his sword and struck me on the head. Before I could utter 'Why do you strike me?' my eldest brother struck me on my shoulder. Both the wounds were severe. I staggered and fell to the ground. At their ease these two merciless persons wounded me all the more and left me bathed in my blood. This dog made a rush at them and they wounded it as well. Then they gave themselves some minor injuries and ran back to the camp bareheaded and barefoot and said, 'Robbers have killed our brother over there. We also got wounded while fighting them. Better we move off quickly from this place, or else they shall soon fall on the caravan and rob us all.' When the people of the caravan heard of the robbers they were scared and marched off. My wife had already heard from me all about the ill treatment my trecherous brothers had meted out to me in the past. Hearing of this incident from these liars she stabbed herself to death.'"

'O dervishes, after Khwaja the dog-worshipper had related all this I broke into tears. He continued, 'Your Majesty, if it were not bad manners, I would have taken off my clothes and shown you my wounded body." With these words he tore off his shirt at the shoulder. Actually, there was not an inch of his skin free from scars. He also took off his turban. There was such a big dent in his skull that a whole pomegranate would fit into it. All the officers of state and others present there shut their eyes as they could not bear the sight.

'"Your Majesty," the Khwaja continued, "when these brothers thought that they had done their work, they went away. My dog and I lay there badly wounded. I had lost so much blood that I had no strength left within me. I lay there unconscious. I do not know how I remained alive.

The Princess of Sarandeep

'"The place where my dog and I lay wounded was on the frontiers of Sarandeep. Not far away from it was a populous city with a big temple in it. The king of that country had a beautiful daughter. Many kings and princes had wasted away in their longing for her. The women of that country did not wear veils. The princess used to go out hunting and enjoy herself with her friends. There was a royal garden near the spot where we lay. With the permission of the king she had come to the garden and as she roamed around she happened to pass by the place where we lay. Some close female friends of the princess who often rode with her came close to me as they could hear me groaning. Seeing me in that condition they rode back to the princess and told her about us. She came there and was moved to see me in that condition. She took pity on me and said to her companions, 'See, if he is still alive.' Two or three attendants dismounted and after examining me said, 'Yes, he is breathing.' At once the princess ordered them to lay me on a carpet and carefully remove me to the garden. There she sent for the royal surgeon and ordered him to attend to me and my dog. She promised him a handsome reward for it. He washed the wounds with spirit, stitched them and applied ointments. He also poured musk into my mouth. The princess remained there and saw to it that I was well attended. Three or four times during the day and then at night she poured broth or sherbet into my mouth. When I regained consciousness I saw the princess and heard her saying in sorrow, 'What heartless tyrant has done this to you? Did he not fear the Great Idol?'

'"The sherbet and broth gave me some strength. After ten days when I opened my eyes I saw lovely damsels around me. It was the court of Indra, as though. The princess stood by my bed. I heaved a sigh and wished to move but I could not because I did not have the strength. The princess with all kindness said, 'O Persian, take it easy. Have no grief. Someone truly callous has wounded you but the Great Idol has helped me heal you. Now you shall be all right.' I swear by God, the One and Incomparable, I fainted to see her beauty. She showered rose water on my face. Within twenty days my wounds had healed. The princess regularly visited and fed me when all others fell asleep.

'"In short, after forty days I felt quite well and took my bath. The princess was pleased and gave the surgeon a good reward. She then got me richly dressed. By the grace of God and with the care and attention of the princess I regained my health. In fact, I had become a bit stout. This dog also had become fat. She wined me and dined me and was pleased to talk to me. I on my part entertained her by narrating interesting tales and anecdotes.

'"One day she asked me to relate to her the events of my past life which I did. It moved her so much that she could not hold back her tears and said, 'I shall now so treat you that you will forget all your past miseries.' I said, 'May God bless you. You have given me a new life. Now I am yours. For God's sake, please always remain kind to me.' She remained with me all night; sometimes her nurse would also stay with her. We told each other stories. When she would depart and I was left alone, I performed my ablutions and secretly said my prayers.

'"Once it so happened that the princess had gone to her father. I was saying my prayers without any fear when the princess suddenly came there saying to her nurse, 'Let us see what that Persian is doing. Is he asleep or awake?' When she did not find me in my room she was surprised and said, 'Where has he gone, eh? I hope he has not fallen in love with someone else.' Looking out for me she came to the place where I was saying my prayers. As she had never seen anyone saying prayers the way I was, she stood there watching me closely. When I had finished and raised my hands in prayer and prostrated myself, she laughed loudly and said, 'This man has certainly gone mad. Look how ridiculous he looks doing all this?' I was a bit alarmed as she laughed. Coming closer to me she said, 'O Persian, what was all this?' Before I could make any reply her nurse said, 'My darling, I understand he is a Muslim and an enemy of the idols *Lāt* and *Manāt*. He worships God the Unseen.' Upon these words the princess rubbed her hands with regret and said in anger, 'I did not suspect at all that he was a Turk and did not believe in our gods. It was because of this alone that he had fallen under the wrath of our Idol. It was a folly on my part to save his life and keep him in my house!' With these words she left. I was disturbed to hear these words. The anxiety as to what she might do to me did not let me sleep. I wept bitterly all night. Three days and nights I passed in anxiety. I couldn't sleep a wink. On the third night the princess, inebriated and followed by her nurse, came to my apartment. She was full of anger and armed with a bow and arrow. She took her seat in the garden and asked the nurse for a cup of wine which she gave her. She drank it and said to her, 'Is that Persian who has fallen under the wrath of our Great Idol still alive, or has he expired?' The nurse replied, 'Darling, he still has some life left in him.' She said, 'He has now fallen from my favour. However, ask him to come out.' The nurse called me. I ran up to her and found that the princess had turned red in anger. I felt as if my soul had departed from my body. However, I paid my respects and stood there with folded arms. She gave me an angry look and said to her nurse, 'If I kill this enemy of our religion with this arrow, will the Great Idol pardon me? You know I have committed a great sin by keeping him in my house and looking after him.' The nurse replied, 'But darling, I don't see any sin in that. You did not know that he was an enemy when you brought him here. You took pity on him and you will be rewarded for your good deed; and for the evil he has done he will be punished by the Great Idol.' On hearing these words she said to the nurse, 'Ask him to sit down.' The nurse signalled and I sat down. The princess took another cup of wine and said to the nurse, 'Give a cup to this wretched fellow too so that he may be easily killed.' The nurse gave me one which I readily drank and bowed down to the princess in respect. She did not look straight at me. When I was a little inebriated I recited some verses to her; one of them said:

> *I am taken by your charms for good;*
> *To what avail, then, will it be*
> *If I am spared my life!*
> *To what avail if one breathes a while*
> *Under the shadow of a sword!*

She smiled hearing this verse and asked the nurse, 'Are you feeling sleepy?' The nurse got the hint and said, 'Yes, darling, I am.' Then she took her leave. After a while, the princess asked me for a cup of wine. I quickly filled and presented it to her. Coyly she took it from me and drank it off. I fell at her feet. With a gentle pat on my back she said, 'You fool, what wrong do you see in our Great Idol that you worship an Unseen God?' I said, 'Kindly try to be just and fair. Just ponder a little. That God alone is adorable who with only one drop of a fluid has created a lovely person like you and has given you such beauty and charm that may make a thousand men mad with passion. What is there in an idol to worship it? It is only a stone which the stone-cutters give a shape and thus cast a snare to trap the fools. Only those whom Satan leads astray consider the created as the Creator. They prostrate before one whom they themselves make. We are Muslims. We adore Him alone who has created us. For those who go astray is hell; and for us, the true believers, is heaven. Only when you have faith in God will you have the delights of heaven and be able to distinguish between truth and falsehood. Only then will you realize that your present belief is false.'

'"These words softened her heart and by the grace of God she said with tears in her eyes, 'Well, teach me your faith.' I recited our creed which she sincerely repeated after me. Thus she renounced her former faith and became a Muslim. I laid myself at her feet. Till the morning she kept repeating the creed and prayed for atonement for her past aberrations. Then she said, 'I have embraced your faith, but my parents are unbelievers still. How can it be helped?' 'You need not worry about that,' I assured her, 'as one sows, so shall one reap.' She said, 'They have engaged me to my uncle's son and he is an idolator. If, God forbid, I am married to him and get pregnant, it will be very bad, indeed. Let us think about it now so that I may be free from fear.' I said, 'What you say is right. Please do whatever you think best.' She replied, 'I will no longer remain here. I will go somewhere else.' 'But how can you escape?' I asked, 'And where shall you go?' She said, 'First you should go leaving me here and stay with other Muslim travellers in the serai and let me know when a ship is to set sail for Persia. I will send my nurse frequently to you for this very purpose. When you let me know of it I shall leave this place and embark with you. Thus shall I free myself from these wretched idolators.' I said, 'My very life for you and your fidelity! But what about the nurse?' She said, 'That's simple. I will give her a cup of strong poison.' So the plan was made and the next day I went to the caravanserai and hired a room. During the separation I lived only on the hope of meeting her again.

'"During the next two months the merchants of Turkey, Syria and Isfahan got together and planned to return by sea. They loaded their cargo on the ship. As we lived together we became familiar with each other. They said to me, 'Won't you come along? How long will you stay in this land of the unbelievers?' I said, 'What is there for me to take to my country? A slave woman, a chest and a dog—that is all that I have. If you could accommodate me in a little room and let me know its price, I shall be at ease and embark with you.' They gave me a cabin and I paid for it.

'"Having secured a cabin I went to the house of the nurse

and said to her, 'Mother, I have come to take leave of you for I am now going to my country. It will be so fortunate for me if you kindly let me see the princess once more.' Reluctantly she agreed. I told her where I would wait for them at night. Then I came back to the serai. I took my chest and bedding and entrusted them to the master of the ship and told him, 'Tomorrow morning I shall bring my slave-girl.' He said, 'But come early as we shall weigh anchor in the morning.' I said, 'All right.'

'"When night set in I went to the place fixed up with the nurse and waited there. When the first quarter of night had passed, the gate of the seraglio opened and the princess appeared in dirty clothes with a casket full of jewels. She gave me the casket and came along. Early in the morning we reached the seaside. We set out on a small boat and reached on board the ship. This faithful dog was with me still. When it was broad daylight we weighed anchor and set sail. We were smoothly sailing forth when we heard a volley of guns from the port. All of us were alarmed. The ship was anchored. We wondered if the Master of Port meant any mischief. All the merchants had beautiful slave-girls with them. They hid them in their chests lest the Master of Port should seize them. I also hid the princess in a chest. Meanwhile, the Master of Port appeared with his men on a small boat and he came on board the ship. Probably the king had learnt of the nurse's death and the disappearance of the princess. Out of prudence and a feeling of shame he did not make public the incidents but he sent orders to the Master of Port saying: 'I understand that the Persian merchants have beautiful slave-girls. I want to buy some for the princess. You should stop them and present all of them before me. Those I like will be paid for and the rest will be returned.'

'"It was because of this that the Master of Port had himself come to our ship. Next to my cabin there was the berth of another person. He too had a beautiful slave-girl hidden in a chest. The Master of Port took his seat on that very chest and began rounding up all the slave-girls. I thanked God in my heart that it had nothing to do with the princess. When all the slave-girls were seated in a boat the Master of Port smilingly asked the owner of the chest on which he was sitting, 'You also had a slave-girl, eh?' A fool that he was, he said, 'By your feet I swear, I alone have not. All of them have hidden their slave-girls in the chests because they feared you.' So the Master of Port began to search all the chests. My chest was also opened and the princess taken out and carried away with the rest. I was highly grieved and said to myself, 'It is quite baffling. I have known nothing but misfortune. I am losing my *life* as though, and God alone knows what treatment the princess will get?' As a matter of fact, I felt so concerned about her that I forgot the danger to my own life. For the whole day and night I prayed to God for her safety. Next morning they brought all the slave-girls back to our ship. All the merchants were happy as each got back his slave-girl. But the princess alone was not among them. I asked them the reason. They said, 'We do not know. Maybe the king has selected her.' The merchants consoled me and said, 'What is done, is done. Do not grieve now. We shall all pool in and give you its price.' I was upset and said, 'I will not go to Persia.' To the boatmen I said, 'Please take me with you to the shore.' They agreed. I left the ship and took my seat in the boat. The dog also followed me.

'"When I reached the port I kept with me only the casket of jewels which the princess had brought. All other things I distributed among the staff of the port. For one month I wandered from street to street in the city in search of the princess. One night I even managed to enter the king's palace secretly to look for her there but could not find any trace of her. I was nearly done to death by this grief. I wandered about like a mad man. Then it occurred to me that my princess could only be in the house of the Master of Port and nowhere else. So I searched round his house to find some way to enter it. I found a sewer big enough for a man to walk through it. An iron grating was fixed at its mouth but I made up my mind to go into the house through it. So I took off my clothes, entered the sewer full of filth and broke open the grating with great difficulty. Thus entering the house I reached the private apartments. I put on the dress of a woman and began to search all around. I heard a voice from a room as if someone was praying to God. I went nearer and found it was the princess, weeping bitterly, prostrating herself and praying to God: 'For the sake of the Prophet and for the sake of his companions and his progeny, deliver me from this country of unbelievers and let the person who showed me the path of Islam come safe to me.' I ran up to her and threw myself at her feet. The princess embraced me and both of us fainted. When we came to I asked what had happened to her. She said, 'When the Master of Port took all the slave-girls to the shore, I prayed to God that my secret might not be disclosed and that your life not be put in danger. The Great Veiler as He is, no one knew that I was the princess. The Master of Port examined all the slave-girls with a view to purchasing some for himself. He chose me and secretly sent me to his house. The rest he carried to the king. When my father did not find me among them he sent back all of them. This whole scheme was made to find me and now he has floated the rumour that the princess is ill. If I am not found in a few days they will announce that I am dead. And so the king will be spared disgrace. But I am now greatly distressed. The Master of Port has bad designs. He wants me to share his bed. I do not agree. So far he seeks my accord, but I wonder how long it will go on like this. On my part, however, I am determined that if he tries to impose himself on me by force, I shall kill myself. But since you have come here I shall think of another plan. If God wills it so, it will be done. Otherwise there seems to be no escape for me.' I asked what it was. She said, 'It can be carried through if you help me.' I said, 'I am always at your service. If you ask me I would even jump into blazing flames or put a ladder to the sky and ascend to the heavens. I would accomplish even the impossible if you say so.' The princess said, 'Go then to the temple of the Great Idol. At the entrance, they take off their shoes. A black carpet is spread there. It is the custom of this country that one who becomes poor and needy sits there and covers himself with that carpet. People who go to worship there give him whatever they can. When he collects some money in three or four days, the priests give him a robe of honour in the name of the Great Idol and see him off. He leaves the place a rich man and no one ever knows who he is. You also go and sit there, cover yourself well with that carpet and do not speak to anyone. After three days when the priests and the idolators give you the robe and want you to leave, you should keep sitting there. When they implore you much tell them: "I do not want money. Nor do I hanker after wealth. I am an oppressed man and I have come here to make a plaint. Better if the Mother of the Brahmins does me justice, or else the Great Idol will look to it and come to my rescue against the person who has wronged me." You should not agree to leave, however much they persuade you, until the Mother of the Brahmins comes to you. She is very old—two hundred and forty years of age. Her thirty-six sons are the chief priests of the temple. She has the favour of the Great Idol and that is why she commands so much respect. All the people, high or low, consider it their privilege to act upon her advice. Holding the hem of her robe tell her: "O Mother, if you do not mete out justice to this aggrieved traveller, I will dash my head before the Great Idol. He will have mercy and intercede with you for me." When she asks you about your complaint tell her: "I belong to Persia. I came here from so far a place to see the Great Idol and I have heard much of your justice. For many days I lived here in peace. My wife had also accompanied me. She is young and quite charming and beautiful. I do not know how the Master of Port saw her. He forcibly took her away from me and has kept her in his house. We Muslims believe that it is right for us to kill a stranger if he sees our wives or takes them away from us, and thus recover our wives, or else we should not take any food, for, as long as that stranger lives, the wife is forbidden to her rightful husband. As I am helpless I have come here to seek justice from you. And I trust justice will be done to me."

'"After the princess had given me all these instructions I took my leave and came out by the same sewer and put the iron grating in its place. At dawn I went to the temple and covering myself well with the black carpet, sat down at the entrance. Within three days a huge amount of gold and silver and fine cloth was heaped up before me. On the fourth day the priests came to me praying and singing devotional songs. They offered me the robe and wished me to leave. I did not agree to it and cried out to the Great Idol to help and protect me and said, 'I have not come here to beg. I have come to seek justice from the Great Idol and the Mother of the Brahmins. Until justice is meted out to me I shall not leave this place.' They went to the old woman and told her what I had said. Then a priest came to me and said, 'Come, the Mother has sent for you.' Covered with that very carpet I went to her apartment. I saw that the Great Idol was placed on a throne studded with rubies, diamonds, corals and pearls. An old woman, dressed in black, sat nearby, reclining regally on cushions placed on a seat with a rich covering of gold. Two boys, about ten or twelve years of age, stood on her right and left. She called me before her. With utmost respect I went forward and kissed the foot of the throne and then held the hem of her robe. She asked me my story. I related to her as the princess had advised me. On hearing it she said, 'Do the Muslims keep their women in seclusion?' I said, 'Yes, God bless your children. It is our ancient custom.' She said, 'Your religion is good. Just now I will send orders that the Master of Port be produced here before me with your wife. I shall give that ass an exemplary punishment so that he may not dare commit such an act again, and that others also may learn a lesson therefrom.' Then she asked her men, 'Who is the Master of Port who dares to take another's wife by force?' They told her his name. On hearing his name she said to the boys standing by her, 'Take this man immediately with you to the king and tell him: "The Mother says it is the warning of the Great Idol that the Master of Port oppresses the people. He has taken the wife of this man by force. His guilt is decidedly great. Let all his property be attached and given to this Turk whom I favour most, or else you shall be destroyed tonight and suffer our wrath."'

'"The two boys came out of the temple and mounted their horses. All the priests followed them, blowing their shells and singing hymns. All the people of the city, high and low, collected the dust from the ground where the two boys put their feet and kissed it as they considered it sacred. In this way they proceeded to the fort. The king got the news. He came out barefoot to receive them. He then conducted them with great respect into the fort, got them seated with him on the throne and asked them, 'What is it that has made you honour me by your visit today?' The two Brahmin boys told him what the Mother had asked them to convey and threatened him with the wrath and fury of the Great Idol. The king said, 'So, this is the case.' He ordered the revenue officials to immediately go and bring before him the Master of Port with the woman so that he might look into the crime and duly punish him. These words disturbed me and I thought, 'This is not well for me, for, if they bring the princess too with the Master of Port, the secret will be revealed and I don't know what will happen to me then.' This thought unnerved me and in my heart I looked up to God. My countenance changed as I trembled and almost fainted with fear and anguish. The boys guessed that I was not pleased with the king's order. They got up in anger and thundered, 'Man, you have gone mad! You are cast away from the favour of the Great Idol. You think we tell a lie that you want to send for them here and ascertain the crime? Now beware, you have provoked the wrath of the Great Idol. We have conveyed the orders. Now be careful, or else suffer the Great Idol's wrath.'

"'These words scared the king. He stood trembling with folded hands before the Brahmin boys. He tried to appease them but the boys would not sit down. Meanwhile, all the nobles present there spoke ill of the Master of Port. They said, 'Indeed, he is a wicked man and a great oppressor. We cannot relate before Your Majesty his many crimes and offences. Whatever the Mother of the Brahmins has conveyed about him is entirely true. How can it be false? It is the verdict of the Great Idol.'

"'When the king found that all had the same opinion about the Master of Port, he regretted what he had said earlier. He gave me a robe of honour and an order written in his own hand under his personal seal. He also wrote a letter to the Mother of the Brahmins. Then he presented many trays of gold sovereigns and jewels to the boys and saw them off.

"'I went back to the temple highly pleased and presented myself before the old woman. Besides the formal address and respectful compliments the king had written: 'On your command this Muslim has been appointed the Master of Port and given the robe of honour. He is now at liberty to put the former

Master of Port to death. This Turk is now also the owner of all his property and wealth and he may dispose of it in any way he likes. I hope I am forgiven.' The Mother of Brahmins was pleased at this. She ordered, 'Let them beat the drums at the temple's drum-house.' She also asked for five hundred soldiers who were good marksmen to escort me with instructions to 'get hold of the Master of Port and hand him over to this Muslim who may put him to death in any way he likes. Also take care that no one except him, who is dear to me, enters the female apartments. Give him all his treasure and wealth. You should return only when he relieves you and you get a letter of approbation from him to that effect.' She then gave me a robe of honour in the name of the Great Idol and granted me leave.

'"When I reached the port a messenger went ahead and informed the Master of Port of my arrival. He was surprised to see me there. I was already full of rage. I drew my sword and severed his head in one blow. I ordered arrested all the officials there—the treasurer and clerks and guards—to be arrested, and took possession of all the papers. I entered the house and met the princess. We embraced each other and wept and thanked God. We wiped off each other's tears. Then I came out and took my seat and gave robes to the officers of the port and reinstated them to their respective posts. To the rest of the staff I gave rewards. I gave presents to the soldiers who had escorted me and rich clothes to the officers and granted them leave.

'"After a week I took with me costly jewels, rolls of brocade, embroidered cloth, shawls and valuable rarities from different lands to present to the king, the nobles, the Mother of the Brahmins and the priests and went to the temple. I placed my presents before the Mother as my offering. She gave me a title and another robe of honour. Then I went to the king and presented a huge sum and valuable gifts. I related to His Majesty the maladministration and the acts of oppression and tyranny of the former Master of Port to justify my act. The king, the nobles and the merchants were pleased at this. The king treated me kindly and before granting me leave gave me a robe of honour, a title and an estate and thus exalted me. When I came out I gave the servants and attendants of the palace so much that all of them praised me and prayed for my prosperity.

'"In short, I was soon well off and lived with ease and comfort in that country after marrying the princess, and I thanked God. All the citizens were happy with my administration. Once a month I went to the temple and also saught the king's audience. The king exalted me more and more till at last he took me as one of his advisers. He wouldn't do anything without consulting me. I led a completely carefree life but God alone knows that I often thought of these brothers of mine and was anxious to know about their welfare.

'"After two years a caravan of merchants arrived from Zerbad on its way to Persia. They wished to proceed by sea. It was the custom that the chief of every caravan presented rarities of different lands to me and as the Master of Port I used to visit them to collect one tenth *ad volerum* duty on their goods in transit and issue them the clearance certificate. So the merchants from Zerbad also came to me and presented valuable gifts. I went to their camp. I saw there two men in rags who brought packages on their heads before me. After my inspection they carried them back. They worked very hard, indeed. I looked searchingly at them and found that they were my own brothers. Out of shame I did not like to see them in that condition. So when I retired to my place I asked my men to bring them to me. When they brought them I gave them new clothes and kept them with me. But these vile beings again made a plot to kill me. One night they stole upon me in my sleep although there were guards at my door. This faithful dog lay under my bed. The moment they drew their swords from their scabbards the dog barked and rushed at them. This woke all the others up. I also woke up and the guards caught them. Everyone cursed and reproached them that in spite of so much kindness shown to them they behaved in that vile manner.

'"Your Majesty, I too was alarmed by now, for as they say: 'For once it may be a fault, twice too, but a third time it means that the man is really base.' So I made up my mind to have them confined. But then I thought that if I had them put in prison, who would look after them? And that they might well do some other mischief. So I put each of them in a cage so that they might always remain before me and not do anything wicked, and that I might also be at rest. As for this dog, I care much for it because it is faithful. An ungrateful man is worse than a faithful animal. This then is the story of my life and I have related it all. Now it is at the sweet will of Your Majesty to put me to death or grant me my life."

'I praised the Khwaja for his righteousness and said, "Now I have no doubt about your goodness and benevolence. Their shameless and base conduct proves the adage that 'a dog's tail remains crooked even if it is buried deep for twelve years." Then I asked him about the twelve rubies in his dog's collar.

The Merchant's Son of Azerbaijan

'The Khwaja said, "May Your Majesty live a hundred and twenty years! Three or four years passed since I had become the Master of Port. One day from my housetop which was quite high, I was watching the sights of the sea and the woods around. All of a sudden there appeared two human figures in the woods. I knew there was no highway there. I looked at them through a glass and found that they had a strange appearance. I sent the guards to call them. When they came I found that one of them was a man and the other a woman. I sent the woman to the princess in the seraglio and called the man before me. He was a young man of twenty or twenty-two years of age who had turned quite dark due to exposure to the sun. His long unkempt hair and uncut nails seemed to suggest that he was a man of the woods. He was carrying a child of three or four years of age on his shoulder and two sleeves of a garment filled with something heavy hung like a big necklace around his neck. I wondered at his condition and asked him, 'Who are you, man? What country do you belong to? And how is it that you are reduced to this condition?' The young man burst into tears and taking off the two stuffed sleeves from around his neck he placed them before me and said, 'I am hungry! For God's sake, please, give me something to eat first. For a long time I have been feeding on leaves and vegetation and I have no strength left within me.' At once I got him bread and meat and wine and he began to eat. Meanwhile, my eunuch brought from the seraglio a number of bags which the young man's wife had been carrying. When they were opened I found they contained gems and precious stones of every kind. Each of them could easily compensate the revenue of a king and each one vied with the others in beauty of shape and brilliance of hue. The entire hall was filled with their light and sparkle."

'"After the young man had eaten and had had something to drink, he looked composed. I asked him, 'Where did you get all these gems and precious stones?' He said, 'My homeland is Azerbaijan. Ever since I was separated from my parents in my boyhood I have known many a hardship; for a long time I have lived like one in a grave; more than once I have escaped from the jaws of death.' I said, 'Young man, let me know the details so that I may follow what you say.' He then related to me this story:

'"My father was a merchant. He used to go on journeys to India, Turkey, China Katay and Farang. When I was ten years old he intended to set out for India and wished to take me with him. My mother and aunts and others said I was yet a child and not old enough to go on a journey but my father would not listen to them and said, "He is old enough to accompany me in my travels. If I don't take him with me now I will carry this desire unfulfilled into my grave. He is a grown-up boy; and if he does not learn now, when will he?" Thus he took me with him and set out.

'"We travelled safely and reached India. There we sold our goods and buying some rarities we went to Zerbad. This was also a safe journey. There too we bought and sold goods and embarked on board a ship to return quickly to our country. After about a month on sea there was a storm. Stormy winds and heavy rains tossed us about. It became all dark from sky to earth. The master and the crew of the ship heaved deep sighs and beat their heads. For ten days we remained at the mercy of the winds and waves. On the eleventh day the ship struck a rock and broke into several pieces. I do not know what became of my father, our servants and our goods. I found myself alone on a wooden plank. For three days and nights it floated at the mercy of the waves. On the fourth day it drifted ashore and with the little strength that was left in me I crawled onto the land. There I could see some fields at a distance. Many people had assembled there. They were dark-coloured and wore no clothes. They were saying something to me which I could not understand. There were some houses nearby. There were gram fields where people parched the gram in the fire that they lit. Perhaps it was their only food. They also gestured to me to eat some. I took a handful of the grams and parching them began to eat. After drinking a little water I fell asleep in a corner of the field. When I woke up after a short while, one of these people came to me and showed me a path. I plucked some green ears of gram and went the way he had shown. It was a vast plain, like the proverbial one of Judgement Day. For four days I went along that path. I ate some gram when I felt hungry. At long last I saw a fort and proceeding further I found it was very high, made of stone and each side about four miles in length. Its stone gate was made of single slab. It was closed and there was a big lock on it. There was no trace of a human being. Going further I saw a hillock, the earth of which was as black as collyrium. I passed over the hillock and saw a big city. It had a boundary wall with many bastions. A river flowed on one side. I reached the gate and reciting the name of God entered the city. I saw a man dressed like the people of *Farang* seated on a stool. When he heard me recite the name of God and saw that I was a stranger he called me to him. I went up to him and paid him my respects. He returned my greetings with kindness. He laid before me some bread and butter, and a roasted chicken and wine and asked me to partake of it. After taking a little of it I fell asleep.

'"When I woke up the night had set in. I washed myself. He again dined me and said, 'My dear boy, relate to me your story.' I told him of my plight. He asked, 'But why have you come here?' I felt annoyed and said, 'Perhaps you have gone mad. After being through that calamity and suffering so much pain I saw a human habitation and so came here and you ask me why I have come here!' He said, 'Well, go to sleep now. Whatever I have to say, I will say tomorrow.'

'"In the morning he said, 'Bring from that small room a

spade, a sieve and a leather bag.' I thought, 'He has fed me but God alone knows what labour he will now put me to!' Anyway, I took the things out and placed them before him. He said, 'Take these things and go to that hillock; dig the earth a yard deep, collect and pass through this sieve whatever you find there. That which does not pass through this sieve, bring to me.' I took the implements and went there. I dug the ground as deep as he had advised. I collected what I found there and put in the leather bag all that could not be made to pass through the sieve. Actually these were all precious stones of different hues. Their brilliance dazzled my eyes. I took a bagful of them to that man. He said, 'Take all that you have brought and leave this place. It is not good for you to stay in this city.' I said, 'You think it is an act of kindness on your part to give me these stones. Of what use will they be to me? I cannot eat them when I am hungry. Even if you give me more of these, they will not help me.' The man laughed at this and said, 'I take pity on you and advise you so, for you also belong to Persia like me. The choice will be entirely yours, of course. But if you are so determined to stay in this city, take my ring with you. When you reach the city's main street you fill find a man with a white beard sitting there. He is my elder brother and resembles me. Give him the ring. He will look after you. I have no jurisdiction over the city. You should act according to his advice or else you may lose your life for nothing.' Taking the ring from him and paying my respects I took my leave and entered the city.

'"It was a city full of grandeur. All the lanes and streets were clean. Men and women were freely buying and selling goods. They were all well-dressed. Enjoying my stroll in the city I reached the main street. It was so thickly crowded that if a saucer were thrown it would have glided on the heads of the people. It was difficult to find the path. When the crowd grew thinner I pushed my way through it and at last found the man I was looking for. He was sitting on a low table and a staff studded with precious stones lay before him. I greeted him and gave him the seal-ring. He gave me an angry look and said, 'Why have you come here? Didn't my foolish brother warn you?' I said, 'Yes, he did. I have come here of my own accord.' Then I related to him my story. He got up and took me to his house. It was like a royal palace with many servants in attendance. He took me to his private apartment and said with affection, 'O son, what a folly you have committed! It is as though you have dug your own grave. Who the wretch would like to come to this accursed city!' I said, 'I have already related to you my circumstances. My fate has brought me here. Now kindly let me know the custom of this place so that I may also know why you and your brother advise me not to stay here.' The kindly old man said, 'The king and the citizens are exceedingly strange. They have an idol in a temple here. From inside the idol, Satan himself tells the name and religion of every visitor. In this way the king comes to know about every traveller who comes here. He then takes him to the temple and asks him to prostrate before the idol. It is well for him if he does it, or else they drown the poor man in the sea. If he tries to escape from the sea his private parts become so long and heavy that he drags them along the ground and is thus unable to walk. This city is accursed. I pity your youth. I have, however, thought of a plan so that you may live and escape the impending doom for some time at least.' I anxiously asked, 'May I know what it is?' He replied, 'I will get you married to the vizier's daughter.' I said, 'But why should the vizier give his daughter in marriage to a poor fellow like me until I embrace their faith. And this I am not going to do.' He said, 'It is the custom of this city that if a person prostrates himself in front of that idol and asks for the hand of even the king's daughter, they will give her in marriage to him to please him even if he is a beggar. They would never disappoint and grieve him. Moreover, I am in the confidence of the King and he favours me. The officers and the nobles also respect me much. Twice a week they go to worship in the temple. They will assemble there tomorrow. I'll take you there with me.' With these words he gave me food and drinks and sent me to bed.

'"Next morning he asked me to accompany him to the temple. There I saw that people came, worshipped the Idol and left. The king and the nobles squatted with the priests on the floor with their heads uncovered. Unmarried girls and boys, as beautiful as the *houris* and *ghilman*, stood in rows all around.

The kind old man said to me, 'Now do as I say.' I agreed and said, 'I will do whatever you tell me to.' He asked me to kiss the king's hands and feet with respect and then hold the vizier's robe which I did. The king asked, 'Who is he and what does he want?' He said, 'This young man is my relation. He has come here from afar to kiss Your Majesty's feet and hopes that the vizier will give his daughter in marriage to him and thus exalt him if the Great Idol and Your Majesty approve it.' The king said, 'He is welcome if he embraces our religion and faith.' Immediately there started the beating of drums in the drum-house of the temple. They gave me a rich robe to wear and then putting a black cord around my neck dragged me to the seat of the Great Idol and made me prostrate before it. Just then a voice issued from inside the Idol which said, 'You, son of Khwaja, it is good for you to be among my worshippers. Now wait and see how I bestow my kindness and favours on you.' On these words all those present there prostrated themselves before it, rolled on the floor and said, 'Of course, thou art the lord, truly so.'

'"In the evening the king along with the vizier rode to the latter's palace. After performing the rites they gave the vizier's daughter in marriage to me and got us settled in a separate house. They also gave me a handsome dowry and said, 'By the command of the Great Idol we have given her in marriage to you.' When I saw her I found she had all the beauty of the legendary Padmini and really looked like a fairy. In the morning after taking my bath I waited on the King. He bestowed on me the robe of marriage and ordered that I should regularly attend his court. After a few days he included me among his counsellors. He was always pleased with me and gave me robes and presents from time to time. I lived in ease and comfort. My wife had brought me plenty of everything including gold and jewels.

'"Two years passed in this manner. My wife got pregnant. When the seventh and the eight months passed, the pains started. The midwife came and a dead child was brought forth. Its poison spread to the mother and she also died. I was mad with grief. I wept by her dead body and all at once the whole house echoed with lamentations and cries as women assembled there. Each one of them struck my head with both her hands, exposed her private parts, and then stood before me and wept. So many women assembled there that I was almost hidden amidst their naked bodies. It was so suffocating there. At that moment someone pulled me from behind by my collar. It was the same old man of Persia who had got me married to the vizier's daughter. He said to me, 'You fool, why do you weep?' I said, 'How cruel that you put to me this question! It is as if I have lost my kingdom. All the joys and comforts of a home are gone, and you ask me why I weep!' Smiling sadly he said, 'Now weep over your own death. Didn't I tell you that your destined death had brought you to this city? And the same has come true. There is no escape for you now.'

'"At last the people led me to the temple. The king and the nobles and all the citizens assembled there. All the wealth and property of the vizier's daughter was placed there and everyone took out of it whatever he pleased and put down its value in money. Thus all her property was converted into money. Precious stones were then purchased with this money and kept in a box. In another chest they kept bread, sweetmeats, meat preparations, dry and green fruits and other eatables. The dead body of my wife was put in another chest. Both the chests were hung across a camel and they mounted me on it and put the box of precious stones in my lap. All the Brahmins walked ahead of the camel, singing hymns and blowing their shells. A huge crowd followed, wishing me good luck. By the same gate through which I had entered the city, I was taken out. The guard I had met earlier wept to see me and said, 'You unfortunate, now you are in the jaws of death! You did not listen to my advice and stayed in the city and now you lose your life for nothing. But you will remember I had already warned you. You can not blame me now.' I was so bewildered at what was going on around me that nothing he said made sense. I couldn't utter a word and just wondered about what was to happen to me. They took me to the same fort whose stone-gate I had seen locked before entering the city. It took several men to unlock and open the gate. Then they carried the coffin and the chest of eatables into the fort. One priest came to me and said, 'Man is born to die one day. This is the way of the world. Now here is your wife, your son and your provisions for forty days. Take it and stay here till the Great Idol is pleased with you.' I was full of rage and wished to curse their idol and the citizens and their customs and give the priest a good beating but the same old man from Persia advised me in his own sweet tongue not to do so. He said, 'Take care, do not utter a single word. If you do, they will burn you immediately. What was destined for you has come to be. Have faith in the mercy of God. He may yet deliver you alive from this place.' In short, leaving me there all alone, they went out of the fort and locked the gate.

"'I wept bitterly at my state and helplessness. I kicked the dead body of my wife and exclaimed, 'You accursed woman, if you were to die in childbirth why did you marry and conceive at all?' I cursed and beat the dead woman till I was exhausted and then sat quietly in a corner. The day advanced and the sun became dreadfully hot. I felt as though my brain would boil and melt. The stench was also killing me. All around me lay the bones of dead bodies and boxes full of precious stones. I gathered some old chests and placed them one upon the other so as to form a shed to protect me from the heat of the sun and the night dew. Then I searched for water. I found a tiny streak of water flowing out of a pot-like mouth in the cut out stones of the wall. Thus I lived for some time on the provisions I had with me. But when these were finished I was much worried and prayed to God. He is so benevolent and kind that soon the gate of the fort opened and they brought another coffin. An old man was also brought with it. When they left him and went away I thought of killing the old man and taking his chest of provisions. Taking the leg of an old wooden chest I went up to him. He was sitting lost in thought with his head on his knees. I crept up on him and gave him such a blow on his head that his brains spilled and he died at once. I took his provisions and lived on them. Thereafter, it became my practice to kill the living person who accompanied each coffin and thus I lived on their provisions.

"'After a long time a young girl was brought with a coffin. As she was quite beautiful I did not have the heart to kill her. When she saw me, she fainted from fear. I kept her provisions with me, but I did not eat them alone. When I felt hungry I took some to her and we ate together. By and by she realized that I did not want to harm her and she feared me less and would often come to my shed. One day I asked her name and inquired about her life-story. She said, 'I am the daughter of the king's Prime Minister and was married to my uncle's son. On the wedding night he had a serious attack of colic pain and he died of it at once. They left me here with his coffin.' Then she asked me about my life. I also related to her my story and said, 'God has sent you here for me.' She said nothing, only smiled. Before long, we had fallen in love. I taught her the basic tenets of Islam and made her recite the creed after me. Then I married her. She became pregnant and a son was born to us. We passed three years in this way. When my wife weaned the child I said to her one day, 'How long shall we live here? Can't we find some way to escape from this place?' She said, 'God alone can help us or else we shall die here one day.' On these words I broke down and wept bitterly till I fell asleep. That night I had a dream. I saw a person in my dream saying to me, 'If you want to get out from this place, get out through the drain.' I woke up with joy and said to my wife, 'Bring to me all the iron rods and nails from the old chests so that we may widen the drain. I would keep the iron rod at the mouth of the drain and strike it hard with stones until I tired myself. After one year's hard labour it was wide enough for a man to pass through. We collected the finest precious stones and stuffed them into sleeves ripped from the dead men's shirts. Taking them with us we crawled out through the drain and thanked God. I took the child on my shoulder and for the past one month we have been travelling through mountains and woods, avoiding the highway for fear. We have lived on grass and leaves. This is my story. Now I have no more strength to speak."

'Khwaja the dog-worshipper continued, "Your Majesty, I pitied him, sent him to the bath and got him dressed well. I made him my deputy. I had many children from the princess but they all died young. One son expired when he was five years old and soon after the princess also died of grief. I was disillusioned. Life without her became unbearable for me and

I decided to return to Persia. With the king's approval I got the young man appointed as Master of Port in my place. In the meantime the king also passed away. I took this faithful dog and all my jewels and money with me and came to Nishapur so that no one might know the story of my brothers. I came to be known as a dog-worshipper. For this reputation I pay double taxes to the king of Persia. Then it so happened that this *merchant's son* (vizier's daughter) arrived there. It is due to him that I have now the honour of kissing Your Majesty's feet."

I asked him, "Is this *young man* not your son, then?" The Khwaja replied, "*He* is not my son, Your Majesty. *He* is one of your subjects but now *he* is my son, or heir, or whatever you like." On hearing this I asked the *young merchant*, "Whose son are you? And where are your parents?" The *young merchant* kissed the ground before me and said, "This humble being is the daughter of Your Majesty's vizier. He has fallen under the wrath of Your Majesty owing to his mention of the rubies that this Khwaja has sewn on his dog's collar. Your Majesty's orders were that if within one year my father was not proved right he would be put to death. On hearing this I disguised myself as a merchant's son and went to Nishapur. God helped me bring the Khwaja here with his dog. Your Majesty has heard all that happened. Now I request that my aged father be released."

'On these words of the vizier's daughter the Khwaja heaved a deep sigh and collapsed. Rose-water was showered on him and when he regained consciousness he said, "Bad luck to me! I undertook this long and hazardous journey in the hope that I would adopt the *young merchant* as my son and write a deed to make him master of all my wealth and property so that my name would live on in this world. But alas, now none of this will come true. A woman, as she is, she has ruined an old man like me. I was snared by her wiles. I feel like a man who performed the necessary rites and left his home to go on a pilgrimage but failed to reach his destination.'

'In short, I took pity on the Khwaja, for his agony and lamentations were unbearable. I called him near me and whispered to him, "Don't feel sad. I shall get you married to her. And if God wishes it so, you shall beget children and they will be your heirs." I comforted him thus and ordered the vizier's daughter to be conducted to the royal palace. I also ordered the vizier to be released from the prison and be brought before me dressed in the robe of honour and exaltation. When the vizier was conducted there, I went up to the far end of the floor to receive him as a mark of respect for his age. I embraced him and reinstated him as my vizier. On the Khwaja also I conferred a high office and gave him an estate. On an auspicious day I married him to the vizier's daughter and in a few years he begot two sons and a daughter. The elder son is now the biggest merchant in my kingdom and the younger one is the Keeper of the Royal Palace.

'O dervishes, I have related all this because I heard the life-stories of two of you last night. Now the other two of you may also please relate your life-stories. Please imagine yourself to be at the same place where you were last night. Take this place to be your abode and myself as your attendant. Please relate without fear and stay here for some time more.'

When the two dervishes found the king so kind to them they said, 'Well, since Your Majesty has been so kind to us, we will both relate our life-stories.'

Adventures of the Third Dervish

The third dervish made himself comfortable and said:

> 'Friends, this is the story of this humble being;
> This is, in fact, what happened to me; listen, please!
> What the King of Love has done to me,
> I relate it all; listen, please!

'This humble being is the prince of Persia. My father, the king, had no other child. I passed my youth playing with my friends at dice and cards and draughts. Or else, I would ride and go out hunting. One day I got my hunting party ready and taking my friends with me rode over the plains. We let loose the falcons and hawks on partridges and fowls and rode quite far away till we reached a really delightful place. For miles together, as far as we could see, it was lush green and red flowers bloomed in profusion. We loosened the reins and cantered along enjoying the delightful sights. Suddenly we saw a black deer. It had a brocade covering on its back and a golden collar studded with jewels and golden bells round its neck. As there was no other animal or man there, it moved about grazing fearlessly. Hearing our horses' hooves ring from afar, it became alert, lifted its head and began to move slowly. I wished to catch it alive. I said to my companions, 'Stay here while I catch it. Please take care, do not come after me.' My horse was very swift. I had chased many a deer riding on it and in spite of their leaps and jumps I had caught them. I put my horse after it. Seeing me chasing it, the deer began to run, taking long leaps; it ran like the wind itself. My horse also galloped fast

117

but it could not keep pace with the deer. It was sweating. My throat too was parched with thirst. Dusk was fast setting in and I did not know how far I had gone or where I was. Finding no other alternative I tricked the deer. Taking an arrow from my quiver I adjusted it in my bow and aiming at its thighs I shot at it in the name of God. The arrow pierced its thigh, yet it limped away towards the foot of the mountains. I dismounted from my horse and chased it on foot. It took to the mountains and I followed. After passing over many slopes I saw a dome. When I arrived there I saw a garden and a spring but the deer had eluded me and disappeared. I was extremely tired. As I washed my hands and feet I heard lamenting cries from inside the dome: "O my child, may this sigh of mine dart and pierce through the heart of him who has struck you with this arrow. May he not taste the fruit of his youth; may God make him a mourner like me." Hearing these words I went to the dome and found a well-dressed old man with a flowing white beard sitting against a cushion and the deer lying before him. He was extracting the arrow from its thigh and cursing the hunter. With respect I joined my hands together and said, "Respected sir, this crime has been unknowingly committed by this humble one. I did not know it was yours. For the sake of God, please forgive me." He said, "You have hurt a dumb creature. If you have done it unknowingly, God will forgive you." I sat down and helped him take out the arrow. Then we applied ointment on the wound and let the deer go. We washed our hands. The old man laid before me whatever eatables he had there. I ate some of them and, tired as I was, lay down on a bed and slept. I was awakened by a wailing sound. I got up and rubbing my eyes found there was neither the old man nor the deer. I was all alone on the bed in an empty room. Looking around in alarm I saw a screen suspended in a corner. I went to it and lifted it. There I saw a low table on which was seated a fairy-like girl, about fourteen years of age and dressed like a European. Her face, flanked by her hair that fell on either side, was like the moon. She was smiling and looked charming and graceful. The old man lay prostrate before her with his head on her feet, weeping bitterly and quite out of his senses. I felt sad to see him in that condition. Then I felt myself lost in the beauty and charm of the girl and fainted. I lay like a dead body on the floor. The old man showered some rose-water on my face. When I recovered, I went to greet the girl. She did not return my greetings, nor did she move her lips to say anything. I said, "O rose-like beauty, what religion will approve of so much pride that you do not even return my greetings:

> *To be reserved in speech is graceful for a beauty, yes;*
> *But not much too much*
> *That even if the lover be dying,*
> *She would not move her lips!*

For the sake of God who has created you, pray say something. Only by chance I happen to be here. One should always be courteous to a visitor." I talked to her but it was no use. Like a statue she sat there, silent. I touched her feet and found them quite hard. I realized then that all that she was formed out of was stone, as if *Āzar* the idol-maker had made her. I said to the old man, the idol-worshipper, "I struck an arrow into your deer's leg but you have planted in my heart the dart of love. Your curse has worked. Now tell me why you cast this spell? Why do you live in the woods and mountains? Relate to me all that has happened to you." When I pressed him much, he said, "Well, it has ruined me. Why do you want to invite your death by wishing to hear it?" I said, "No excuses old man. Come to the point; tell me all, otherwise I shall kill you!" On my persistence he said, "Young man, may God guard every one from the fire of love! It brings only pain and suffering. For love alone a woman commits *sati*, burns herself on her husband's pyre. Everyone knows how this love ruined Farhad and Mujnun and brought their end. What will you gain by listening to my story? You will only leave your home and country, your property and wealth to wander about, getting nothing out of life." I said, "Hold your tongue; no more words. Keep this feigned friendship to yourself. Take me as your enemy now and if you hold your life dear, plainly relate to me your story." Realizing that there was no escape for him, with tearful eyes he said, "Well, here then is the story of this unfortunate being:

Nu'mān the Merchant-Traveller

"I am Nu'mān, a merchant-traveller. Consider my old age; I have been to all the parts of the world in connection with my business. I have also been received by many a king. One day I thought, 'I have been to the four corners of the world but I have not visited the Island of Farang, nor yet seen its king, soldiers and citizens. I do not know their manners and customs. Once at least I must go there.' So, after consulting my friends, I decided to go there. I took with me rarities which would sell there, and formed a caravan of merchants. We boarded a ship and set sail. The wind was favourable and in a few months we reached Farang and chose a city to stay in. It was a city full of grandeur; no other city could match it. Every street and lane had well-built roads kept clean and sprinkled with water. Not a straw could be seen, much less any dirt or filth. The buildings were of various colours. At night the streets were lit by lamps arranged in rows on either side. The well-laid out gardens on the outskirts were full of fruits and flowers of rare species were in profusion. Such fruits and flowers could perhaps only be seen in the Garden of Eden. In short, enough cannot be said in praise of that city.

"Our arrival there became the talk of the city. A chamberlain mounted on a horse and followed by his retinue came to our caravan and asked the merchants about their chief. They brought him to me. I received him with respect and we exchanged greetings. I offered him a seat on a rich carpet and cushions to lean against. Then I asked him the reason for his kind visit. He said, 'Our princess has come to know that your merchants have rare merchandise to sell. She has asked me to take them to her. So, please come and bring with you the goods that you consider worthy of her, and thus have the honour to be in her audience.' I said, 'Please excuse me today for I am too tired. Tomorrow I shall present myself. I will lay before her whatever goods I have and she may take whatever she pleases. After making the appointment I presented him scents and betels and saw him off. I called all the merchants and collected from them whatever rarities they had. I took mine as well. Next morning, taking all that with me I reached the royal seraglio. The gate-keeper sent word of my arrival. He was ordered to conduct me in. The same chamberlain came and led me in with all courtesy and friendly discourse. First we went through the apartments of the private attendants of the princess. My dear friend, you won't believe me but I saw there an astoundingly beautiful sight. The beautiful female attendants seemed to be fairies shorn of their wings. I would stare whenever I got a chance. I felt faint and with great difficulty I supported myself and reached the princess. As I glanced at her my limbs trembled and I almost collapsed. However, I managed myself and made a salutation. Beautiful women with their arms folded stood in rows on the right and left. I laid before the princess a variety of jewels and fine cloth and other rarities. She liked them as they lay before her arranged in so many trays. The things were then entrusted to the keeper of the royal house and she said to me, 'These shall be paid for tomorrow as per your list.' I bowed low in respect to her. I was much pleased with the thought that I would have another opportunity to go there the next day. When I came out after taking my leave, I kept mumbling incoherently. In this state I returned to the serai but was not yet my own self. My friends asked me much but I only said, 'It's all due to the heat and exertion of travelling so far.' In short, I passed that night restlessly tossing about in my bed.

"Next morning I again presented myself there. I entered the palace with the same chamberlain. It was the same scene that had dazzled me the day before. When the princess saw me, she dismissed all others. When she was alone, she went to her private apartment and called me there. When I went there she asked me to sit. I bowed in respect and sat down. Then she asked, 'How much profit do you expect on the goods you brought?' I replied, 'I only wished to have the honour to see you and God has granted it. Now I have got all that I had wished. I have acquired the prosperity of both the worlds. The prices, as given in the manifest, are one half cost and one half profit.' She said, 'No, no. You shall be paid whatever prices you have given in your list. You may get even more as a reward if you could do one thing for me. Shall I say it?' I said, 'It will be most fortunate for me if all my life is spent in your service. With all pleasure I shall do it.' On hearing these words she called for her ink-stand. She wrote a note and put it in a small purse of pearls. Wrapping the purse in a fine silk scarf she entrusted it to me. She also gave me as her mark a ring she had on her finger and said, 'There, at the other end of the city, is a big garden known as *Dilkushā*. See the superintendent there, Kaikhusrau by name. Give him this ring, convey my good wishes and ask for a reply to this note. But come back quick. For this work I shall give you a reward you will appreciate only after you get it.'

"I took my leave and went along inquiring the way to the garden. I had gone three miles or so when I saw it. As I proceeded further, an armed man caught me by my arm and took me to the garden gate. I saw there a young man with the looks of a lion sitting with an air of dignity on a seat of gold. He had on an armour like that of David, with steel breastplates and a steel helmet. Five hundred young men armed with shields and swords and bows and arrows stood before him in rows, ready to carry out his command. I bowed in respect to him and gave him the ring. Paying him many compliments by way of flattery I showed him the silk scarf and told him that I had brought a note from the princess. The moment he heard this he bit one of his fingers with his teeth in anguish. Striking his head with his hand, he said, 'Your death has brought you here, perhaps. However, go now into the garden. Amidst the cypresses you will find a young man hanging in an iron cage. Give him the note, take his reply and return quickly.'

"I immediately went into the garden. Ah, what a garden it was! I felt I had entered the Garden of Eden. There were beds and beds of flowers of different hues in bloom. Fountains were playing and birds were singing. I saw a handsome young man chained inside a cage. I bowed my head in respect, then gave him the sealed note through the bars of the cage. He opened and read the note and with fondness inquired about the princess. We had not yet finished our talk when a troop of black soldiers appeared and fell on me from all sides with their swords and spears. What could a single unarmed man do? In a moment I was severely wounded and lay unconscious on the ground. When I regained consciousness, I found myself on a cot being carried by two soldiers on their heads. They were talking to each other. One of them said, 'Let us throw this dead body on the ground here. Let dogs and crows eat it.' The other said, 'But if the king inquires and comes to know of it, he will bury us alive and send our families to be crushed in a mill. Is our life such a burden to us that we should act so foolishly?'

"Hearing them talk like this I said to those two, Gog and Magog, 'For God's sake, take pity on me. I have yet a departing spirit within me. Do whatever you like after I am dead. The dead are always at the mercy of the living. Please tell me what happened to me. Why have they wounded me? And who are you? Pray do tell!' They took pity on me and said, 'The young man confined in the cage is the nephew of the king of this country. His father had the throne. On his deathbed he said to his brother, 'My son, who is heir to my throne, is yet too young and immature. You should look after the affairs of the state with diligence and care. When he comes of age, marry your daughter to him and make him the Master of the Empire and the Royal Treasury.' When he passed away his younger brother ascended the throne. But he did not carry out the will of the late king. He floated the rumour that this nephew of his had gone mad and confined him in a cage. He has placed such strict guards on all four sides of the garden that no one can enter it. Several times he has given him strong poison too but life is stronger and the poison did not work. The princess and this prince are mistress and lover. She is restless at home and he in the cage. To him she sent a love note through you. The spies at once took the news to the king. A body of black soldiers was ordered to arrest you. They treated you thus. Then he asked his vizier to think of some plan to kill the young prisoner. The vizier, ungrateful as he is, has persuaded the princess to kill that innocent prince in the presence of the king.'

"I said to them, 'Let me see this scene at least before I die.' They conceded to my request and with the two soldiers I, though badly wounded, went to the scene and we quietly hid ourselves in a corner. We saw the king seated on the throne and the princess holding a naked sword in her hand. The prince was taken out of the cage and made to stand before them. The princess, who was to be the executioner, came forward with the naked sword in her hand to kill her lover. When she came closer she threw away the sword and held the prince to her bosom. The prince, her lover, said to her, 'I am willing to meet my death this way. I have always wished for thee in this world, and there in the next too I shall wish for thee.' The princess said, 'It was only a trick to see you.' The king was much annoyed at this and reproached the vizier and said, 'So you brought me here to witness this scene!' The guards separated them and took the princess to the seraglio. The vizier, much enraged, took the sword and charged at the poor prince to kill him in one blow. He was about to strike when an arrow, from where it came nobody knew, pierced his forehead, splitting it in two and he fell dead on the ground. Seeing this the king hurriedly went into his palace. The young prince was put back into his cage and carried to the garden. I also came out of my hiding place. A man came there who took me to the princess. Seeing me wounded she immediately sent for a surgeon and ordered him to help me recover quickly. She also told him, 'This is a test of your skill. The more devotedly you attend to him the higher the reward you will get from me.' The surgeon cured me within forty days and letting me have my bath of health took me to the princess. The princess asked me, 'Are you all right now?' I said, 'With your kind attention I have completely recovered.' She gave the surgeon a robe of honour and a large sum of money, much more than she had promised, and gave him leave.

"With my servants and friends who had accompanied me I left that country. When we reached this place I told them to return to their country. I erected this building on this hill and got a statue of the princess installed here. I richly rewarded my servants and slaves according to their ranks and relieving them from my service I said to them, 'Leave food that will sustain me so long as I live, otherwise you are free in every way.' They faithfully provide me with whatever I need and I quietly worship this statue. This is going to be my sole occupation for the rest of my life. This is my life-story."

'O men of God, having heard this story I put on a shroud

and set out to fulfil my earnest desire to see Farang. I wandered about over mountains and in the woods for a long time and those exertions enfeebled me like Majnun and Farhad. At long last my earnestness took me to the same city where Nu'mān the merchant had been. Like a mad man I wandered about in the streets and lanes. Most of the time I stayed near the seraglio of the princess but found no opportunity to see her. It was really a vexing situation that I should not get the very thing for which I had set out and suffered so many hardships.

'One day as I stood in the main street I saw that all of a sudden people began to run and shopkeepers left after hurriedly closing their shops. In a moment it became a deserted place. Then I saw a young man rushing out from a corner of the street. He was like Rustam in appearance and roared like a lion. With a helmet on his head, an armour on his body and a pair of pistols in his girdle he came brandishing a long sword in his hand and muttering something to himself like an inebriated person. Two slaves dressed in broadcloth and bearing a hearse covered with costly velvet on their heads followed him. I made up my mind to go along with them. Whosoever saw me advised me not to do so, but I did not heed them. As the young man proceeded towards a grand mansion I followed him. Turning around, he was about to charge and cut me in two when I urged him on oath to do it and said, "I myself wish the same. I forgive you my blood. Relieve me from the misery of this life for I am disgusted with it. I voluntarily present myself before you. Do not delay." Seeing me so determined to give my life up, God filled his heart with compassion for me. He cooled down and with kindness asked me, "Who are you?" I replied, "Please sit down, I will tell you everything. Mine is quite a long story. I am desperate because I am stricken with love."

On hearing these words he put down his arms and took off his armour. After washing, he ate his meal and gave some of it to me. When we had finished, he said, "Now tell me what has befallen you." I told him of what had happened to Nu'mān the merchant-traveller and the princess and my meeting with him. He wept when he heard all this and said, "Curse be on this love; how many people it has ruined! However, the cure of your affliction seems to be with me. Maybe through the efforts of this guilty being you might fulfil your wish. Now you should not worry. Be at ease." He then ordered the barber to dress my hair and let me have a bath. One of his slaves brought clothes for me. Then he said to me, 'The coffin which is here before you contains the dead body of the prince who was confined in the iron cage. Another vizier killed him by a trick. The prince is blessed because he was innocent. I am his foster-brother. I slew that vizier and wanted to kill the king too, but he begged mercy and swore that he was innocent. Considering him to be a coward I spared him his life. It has been my practice since then to take this hearse out through the city on the first Thursday of every moon and thus mourn the death of the prince." His words relieved me, for I thought that if he so willed, I would fulfil my wish. God is gracious, indeed. How so true: if God favours, all goes well.

'When it was evening and the sun had set, the young man replaced one of the slaves carrying the coffin with me and thus took me with him. He said, "I am going to the princess and will plead for you as much as I can but you should not say anything; you keep silent and listen." I said, "I shall do what you say. May God preserve you for you have taken pity on me." We went to the royal garden. There I saw an octagonal marble platform in the lawns. A canopy of white brocade with a fringe of pearls was made over it on poles studded with diamonds. A seat set with precious stones and with cushions big and small covered with brocade was also provided. The hearse was placed there. We, the two bearers, were asked to sit under a tree.

'After a short while the light of a flambeau appeared. Then the princess arrived there followed by female attendants. She looked sad and angry. She took her seat under the canopy. The foster-brother of the prince stood before her with folded arms. Keeping his proper distance he sat down on the far end of the floor. After praying for the dead prince he had a word with the princess. I listened with attention. Finally he said, "May God preserve you, the Prince of Persia heard of your goodness and beauty and excellence. He abandoned his princedom like Ibrahim Adham and has come all the way here after facing many difficulties. As they say, 'O good God, in Thy path the pilgrim left the city of Balkh,' he has left his country and has been wandering about in this city in great distress. He recklessly followed me without caring for his life. I scared him with my sword but he bowed before me and entreated me on oath to strike him without delay for he wished just the same. He is thus firm in his love for you. I have tested and found him sincere. That is why I have mentioned him to you. It will not be too grent an inconvenience, I hope, if a person like you who fears God and loves justice, treats him kindly as he is a stranger here." The princess said, "Where is he? No harm if he is really a prince. Let him come." The foster-brother of the deceased prince came to me and took me to her. I was so overjoyed to see her that I was stupefied. The princess left shortly afterwards and the foster-brother of the prince came back. When we reached his house he said, "I related to the princess all your circumstances as you had told me and pleaded for you. You may now go there every night and enjoy her company." Out of gratitude I fell at his feet. He helped me up and clasped me in his arms.

'All day I counted the hours and waited until evening so that I might go to the princess. When night set in, I took leave of the foster-brother of the prince and went to the royal garden. I sat down on the marble platform. An hour or so later, the princess arrived, followed by a private female servant, and took her seat under the canopy. It was sheer good luck that I had lived to see the day. I kissed her feet. She helped me up and embraced me and said, "Consider it a Godsend opportunity and do what I say. Take me to some other country." I replied, "Let us go then." After this short conversation both of us left the garden. But we were so excited and overjoyed that we lost our way. We just went along but knew not where we were going. The princess got angry and said, "I am tired now. Where is your house? Get there quickly. Or else you should know what we may have to face. My feet have grown sore. Any moment now I may collapse." I said, "My servant's house is nearby. We shall soon reach there. Please bear with me and come along." I told a lie but in fact I myself was worried about where to take her. Just then I saw a door across the road that was locked. I broke the lock and we entered the place. It was a fine house with carpets well-spread and flasks of wine well-arranged. Bread and roasted meat were stocked in the kitchen. As we were extremely tired we took a bottle of Portuguese wine each and some roasted meat and passed the night enjoying ourselves.

'In the morning there was a furore in the city as the news spread that the princess had disappeared. Announcements were made in every street and lane, and female spies and bawds and messengers were sent all over to find her. Royal guards were posted at all the city gates. Strict orders were issued not to let anybody leave the city without royal permission. It was also announced that whoever brought news about the princess would be given a robe of honour and a thousand gold sovereigns as a reward.

'The bawds combed the whole city and went into every house. It was sheer misfortune that I had forgotten to shut the door. An old hag, like the proverbial devil's aunt, may God blacken her face, with a rosary in her hand and a veil on her face, found the door open. She entered the house and standing before the princess raised her hands to bless her, saying, "May God preserve you long, married woman, and may God preserve your bread-earner and his honour. I am a poor beggar widow and have a daughter in an advanced stage of pregnancy. She has gone into labour. But I have no means to get even a little oil to light our lamp, far less the food for her. If she passes away how can I arrange for her coffin and burial? And if she gives birth to a child how shall I pay the midwife for her services? How shall I provide for her the special food during her maternity period? It is two days now since she last ate anything. O my good lady, give something for her to eat that she may bear a drink of water." The princess took pity on her. She called her near and gave her four loaves, some roast meat and a ring which she had on her little finger and said, "You may sell it and get her some jewels and don't worry too much. You may visit us again whenever you like. You are always welcome."

'That old wretch of a woman got what she wanted and left giving false blessings to the princess. She threw the loaves and

meat at the door but kept the ring with her as it proved that
the princess was there. Now, as God would preserve us from
the impending trouble, the master of the house arrived just
then. He was a brave soldier. Mounted on his horse he had a
spear in his hand and the body of a deer fastened to his saddle.
He was enraged to see the lock broken and the door open and
that old hag coming out of it. Catching hold of her by her hair
he dragged her into the house. He tied her feet and hung her
upside down from the branch of a tree. She died at once of
agony and pain. We got frightened to see him and trembled
in our hearts. Seeing us alarmed, he comforted us and said,
"How imprudent of you to do all this and keep the door open."
The princess said with a smile, "The prince said that this was
the house of his slave and persuaded me to stay here." With
respect the soldier said, "The prince was right because all the
people being their subjects are the slaves of kings. The very
life and prosperity of the people depend upon their benevolence
and protection. Without doubt I am your slave, indeed. But
reason demands that the secret be kept. My dear prince, it is
highly fortunate for me in this world and the next that the
princess and you have honoured me by coming to my poor
abode. I shall lay down even my life for you. Never shall I
withhold my life or property from your service. Rest assured
and live comfortably here; now there is no danger. Had this
vile bawd gone out safely from here she might have brought
us trouble. Live here carefree as long as you please. Kindly let
this slave know whatever you may require, and I will get it for
you. Let alone the king, even the angels would not know that
you are here." The brave soldier thus comforted us. I said,
"Well, you are a brave man, indeed. We shall return your
kindness whenever we are able to do it. What is your name?"
He said, "This slave is known as Behzad Khan.' In short, he
devotedly served us and we lived comfortably there for six
months.

'One day I thought of my parents and felt sad. Behzad
Khan guessed my feelings. Joining his hands together he stood
respectfully before me and said, "Kindly tell me if there is any
slackness on my part." I said, "For God's sake! You have looked
after us so well that we have lived in this city as safe and secure

as children in the mother's womb. Our acts have made everyone our enemy. How could we find anyone to stay with even for a while? May God preserve you, you are really great." He said, "If you are tired of this place I may safely conduct you wherever you please." I replied, "If only I could reach my country, and see my parents. I am all right here but God knows how they are. I have got what I wished and left my country for. Now I must go back to them. They do not know whether I am dead or alive. God alone knows what suffering they might have endured." The soldier said, "Very true, let us set out then." He brought a Turkish horse for me which could go hundred miles a day, and a swift but docile mare for the princess and got us mounted on them. Then he put on his armour, armed himself, mounted his horse and said, "I'll go ahead. You please follow me without any fear." When we reached the city gate he bellowed and broke the lock with his axe. He rebuked and challenged the guards with these words: "You bastards, go and tell your master that Behzad Khan is openly taking his Princess Mehr Niqar and Prince Kamgar who is your son-in-law. Tell him that if he has any pretensions to her he should come and take her from me if he dares. He should not say afterwards that I secretly carried her away and that he did not know of it. Or else he should stay put in his fort and relax." This news soon reached the king. The vizier and the general were ordered to get hold of 'the three villains and produce them dead or alive' before the king. A huge body of troops appeared in no time and the dust created an unnatural darkness from earth to sky. Behzad Khan hid us behind a gate on a bridge which was as big as the twelve-gate bridge or the one at Jaunpur. He spurred his horse and turned towards the troops. He roared like a lion and rushing his horse pounced on them. The whole body of troops was dispersed like scum on water and he penetrated deep into their ranks and cut off the heads of the two chiefs. When the chiefs were killed the troops completely dispersed for, as they say: 'all depends on the head; when it is gone all is gone', or 'when the seed-vessel cracks the grains are scattered all over.' The king himself came over there to reinforce the troops with a large body of armed men. On him also Behzad inflicted a crushing defeat. The king fled. It is true that victory is God's gift but it may be said that even Rustam could not have shown such bravery as Behzad Khan had shown in that battle.

'When he made sure that it was all safe and that no one could pursue us he confidently came to the place where he had hidden us and thus we moved further on. Once you set out, the journey becomes short. So, in a short time I reached my country with them. I sent a letter to the king, my father, informing him of my safe arrival. He was happy and thanked God for my safe return. He got a new lease of life as a withered plant is revived by water. He took the nobles of his court with him and came to the banks of the river to receive me. The Master of the Seas was ordered to arrange for boats to carry us across. I saw the king and those who accompanied him from the opposite bank and grew eager to kiss his feet. I plunged with my horse into the river and making a dash through it presented myself before him. With fatherly affection he clasped me to his breast.

'But in the meantime there was a mishap. The horse on which I rode was perhaps the colt of the mare on which the princess rode, or perhaps they had previously been together for, seeing my horse plunge into the river, the mare also plunged itself into it with the princess and began to swim. The princess became nervous. She pulled at the the reins. The mare was tender-mouthed; it turned over. The princess struggled but to no avail. She was drowned with the mare. Behzad Khan mounted his horse and dashed into the river to rescue the princess but he was caught in a whirlpool. He struggled hard against it but could not push himself out to the bank. He too sank with his horse. Seeing all this, the king sent for the big nets and got them thrown into the river. The boatmen and divers were also ordered to look for their bodies. They searched and searched for them in the whole river, deep down to its bottom, but neither their bodies nor those of the horse and the mare were found.

'O men of God, this mishap made me mad. I gave up the mundane cares of the world, property, wealth and all, and wandered about from place to place crying:

All that the poor eyes can do
Is to see the joys, to see the griefs.

Had the princess disappeared or even died, I could have ventured out in search of her, or could have borne the loss with fortitude. But she was drowned before my very eyes. I could do nothing except think of drowning myself so that I might meet my mistress in death. With this determination I stepped into the same river one night till the water rose to my neck. As I was about to take another step forward and drown myself, the veiled rider who gave you the good news appeared there and held me by my arm. He comforted me and said, "The princess and Behzad Khan are safe and secure. Why are you throwing away your life for nothing? It is the way of the world. Don't be despairing of God's grace. If you remain alive, you will meet both of them one day. You should go towards Turkey. Two other grief-stricken dervishes have already gone there. When you meet them, you shall get what you wish." Friends, this is the story of my life; and I am here now on the advice of that great guide and have the honour to be with you. I firmly hope that each of us will now be able to fulfil his heart's desire.'

Adventures of the Fourth Dervish

With eyes full of tears the fourth dervish began to relate his life-story with these words:

'Listen to the tale of my helplessness;
With attention, please, hear it all!
What caused my ruin and why did I come here?
Listen, I will tell the reason why!

'God be our guide, this humble being in this poor state before you is the son of the Emperor of China. I was brought up in luxury and educated well. I did not know the good or the evil of the world and thought that my life would pass carefree in the same way. But then the sad event of my father's death took place. Before he passed away, he sent for his younger brother, my uncle, and said to him, "I am now going to depart forever and leave behind my empire, wealth and all. Please behave like an elderly counsel after me and act upon my will. Till the prince who is heir to my throne comes of age and is able to look after his affairs, please act as his regent and make sure that his subjects and army are not ruined and spoiled. When the prince comes of age, give him the throne and advise him well in the affairs of the kingdom. Marry him to your daughter, Roshan Akhtar. You may then retire from the government. Thus the kingdom will remain within our family and it will not be disturbed.' He passed away soon after and my uncle became the king and began to rule. He ordered that I should be brought up in the seraglio and not be allowed to come out until I came of age.

133

'So, until I was fourteen I was brought up there among the princesses and their private female attendants and I rejoiced with them. As they say: 'the world lives on hope', so I was happy with the thought that I would be married to my cousin and that I would shortly get the throne. Often I would go and spend time in the company of Mubarak, a black slave who had grown up in my father's service. My father had great trust in him. He was happy to see me growing up and would way, "Praise be to God, you are now grown up, my prince. If God wills it so, your uncle will soon act according to the will of your late father. He will leave you the throne of your father and give his daughter in marriage to you and will retire."

'One day it so happened that a slave-girl slapped me in my face without any cause. The marks of her five fingers remained on my cheek. With tearful eyes I went to Mubarak. He clasped me to his breast and wiped off my tears with his sleeves and said, "Well, let me take you to the king. Maybe he shows affection on seeing you and considering you mature enough, may give you what is your right." Immediately he took me to my uncle who showed me much affection in his court and asked me, "Why are you sad? How is it that you are here today?" Mubarak replied, "He has something to say to Your Majesty." On hearing this my uncle himself said, "Now we should marry this young man." Mubarak said, "It will be most advisable and blessed, Your Majesty." Immediately my uncle sent for the astrologers and asked them to work out the most auspicious day for our marriage. Acting on the king's wily orders they made their calculations and said, "The whole of this year is not suitable, Your Majesty. Not a single day in any of the months appears auspicious. Let this whole year pass in peace, the year following seems to be most auspicious." Looking towards Mubarak the king said, "Take the prince to the seraglio. If God wills it so, I shall give this trust back to him. Let him rest assured and attend to his studies." Mubarak paid him his respects and took me back to the seraglio.

'Two or three days later I went to Mubarak. When he saw me he burst into tears. I was surprised and said, "What is it? I hope all is well. Why are you weeping?" A well-wisher as he was and as he truly loved me, he said, "Alas, I took you to that tyrant the other day. Had I known this, I wouldn't have done it!" Alarmed, I asked him, "Well, what harm was there in my going to him? Pray tell me, please!" He said, "All the nobles and viziers and officers of state of your father's time were pleased to see you. They thanked God that you had grown up and come of age. They said, 'Our prince is now able to rule. In a few days he will get what rightly belongs to him. He will do us justice and favourably consider our past services.' This news reached your uncle, the faithless one, and it went through his breast like a serpent. He called me in private and said, 'Mubarak, kill the prince by some trick and relieve me from this nagging fear. Only then will I feel secure." Ever since I heard these words I have been greatly disturbed. Your uncle has become your deadly enemy.' When I heard this I almost died and fell at his feet for fear of my life and said, "For God's sake, save me by any means. I don't covet the throne." A faithful slave as he was, he lifted my head and clasping me to his breast said, "Don't get disheartened. Life is always like that. I have already thought of a plan. If it goes well, we have not to worry at all; you will be saved and you shall have your desire fulfilled as well."

'Comforting me thus, he took me with him to the place where the late king, my father, used to stay. This restored my confidence. There I saw a chair. He asked me to help him remove it. Then he rolled the carpet and began to dig the floor till I saw a window underneath which was locked. He called me near him. I became convinced in my heart that he had dug the floor to bury me there after killing me. I saw my death before me. Repeating the creed to myself I quietly and slowly went up to him. Through the window I saw a building with four rooms. In every room there were ten large vases of gold suspended by chains. On the mouth of each vase there was a brick of gold on which was placed the figurine of a monkey studded with precious stones. In all there were thirty-nine vases in the four rooms. Another vase was also there full of gold sovereigns but it had neither the figurine nor the brick of gold on it. I also saw a cistern there full of precious stones. I asked Mubarak, "What is all this, my dear old grand man? And what is this place? And of what use are they?" He said, "The figurines of monkeys you see here have a story behind them. In his youth your father had made friends with Malik Sadiq, the king of the djinn and they used to visit each other. Once a year your father paid him a visit and stayed with him for a month. He carried with him different kinds of scents and perfumes and rarities from this country as presents for him. Each time he took his leave, Malik Sadiq used to give him the figurine of a monkey studded with precious stones. Our king would place them in these underground rooms. No one except me knows of this. Once I said to him, 'You Majesty, you take rarities and perfumes worth thousands of rupees as presents but bring only the figurine of a monkey in stone! What is the use of all this?' He smiled at my query and said, 'Beware, do not disclose it to anyone. Each of these lifeless figurines has a thousand powerful demons at its command. But until I have forty such figurines with me, they are worth nothing and can be of no use.' So only one monkey-figurine more was all that was needed when the king passed away. Thus all his labour proved fruitless and produced no results."

'"My dear prince, when I saw you helpless I thought of these figurines. I am now determined to take you somehow to Malik Sadiq and tell him of your uncle's callousness. Maybe he still remembers his friendship with your father and may give you one more figurine of a monkey that is needed to complete the number. With their aid you may get your empire and reign in peace over China. Also, you will escape the danger to your life. And even if nothing comes of it, I cannot think of any other plan to rescue you from your uncle's tyranny." Hearing all this I said to him, "You are the master of my life now. Do what you think best for me." After comforting me he went to the market to buy some scents and perfumes and other things to present to Malik Sadiq.

'The next day he went to my uncle who was like the second Abu Jahal, and said to him, "O protector of the world, I have thought of a plan to kill the prince. If you please, I may relate it." That wily one was pleased and asked him to describe his plan. Mubarak said, "To put him to death here will bring you a bad name. I will take him to the woods, kill him and return after burying him there. No one will ever know what has happened to him." On hearing Mubarak's plan he said, "Excellent! I only want that he be put to death. The very thought that he is alive disturbs me. If you relieve me of this worry, you will get much in return. Take him anywhere and finish him in any way and bring me the good news."

'Having thus assured my uncle, the king, Mubarak took me along with him and we left the city at midnight with a lot of presents for Malik Sadiq, the king of the djinn. We went towards the north and kept on proceeding for one full month. One night, as we were going along, Mubarak said, "Thank God, we have reached our destination." "What do you mean?" I asked. "My dear prince," he replied, "don't you see the army of the djinn?" I said, "I see no one except you." Mubarak took out a little solomon-collyrium and applied it on my eyelids. The moment he did that, I could see the djinn and his people and the tents. All the djinn were good-looking and well-dressed. Recognizing Mubarak, they all embraced him and looked happy to see him there. We thus reached the royal tents. They were well-lit. Seats of different kinds were arranged in double rows. Men of learning and dervishes, nobles and viziers and officers of state were seated on them. Guards and macebearers, servants and other attendants stood there with folded arms to carry out the orders. A throne studded with precious stones was placed in the centre. Malik Sadiq, the king of the djinn, sat there reclining on cushions majestically. He had a crown on his head and wore a dress of pearls. I went up to him and paid my respects. With all kindness he asked me to take my seat. Dinner was ordered. When it was over, Malik Sadiq asked Mubarak about me. Mubarak said, "His uncle now reigns in his father's place and he has become his deadly enemy. That is why I have run away from there and brought him with me before Your Majesty. He is an orphan and actually the throne belongs to him. But no one can do anything unless one finds a patron to support him. He may get what is by right his only if Your Majesty helps him. Kindly remember the services of his father to you and come to his rescue. Please give him the fortieth figurine of a monkey to complete the number so that he may

with their aid get what is rightfully his and always pray for
Your Majesty's life and prosperity. He has no one to seek help
from except Your Majesty."

'On hearing all this Malik Sadiq thought for a while and
said, "You are right. I remember the great services of the late
king and his friendship with me. I realize the prince is helpless.
He is ruined and deprived of his father's empire. He has come
here to seek our protection and help. I realize all this. And you
will not find me wanting in generosity. I shall not let him go
emty-handed. But presently I am preoccupied with another
work; I have to get it done. If he does it and does not deceive
me, if he does it honestly and stands the test, on my word I
shall treat him as more than a king and give him whatever he
may wish from me." Joining my hands in respect to him I said,
"This humble servant will do all he can to serve Your Majesty.
I will put my heart and soul in any work assigned to me. I
shall do it with utmost care and diligence and as nicely as I
can and thus consider myself most fortunate in this world and
the next." He said, "Look here, you are still a boy. I say it
again lest you should deceive me and thus bring trouble to
yourself." I said, "God and the good fortune of Your Majesty
will make it easy for me. I shall accomplish it as best as I can
and not belie your trust in me."

'Reassured, Malik Sadiq called me near him. Taking out a
piece of paper from his pocketbook, he showed it to me and
said, "Find the girl whose portrait this is wherever she may be
and bring her to me. When you meet her, tell her at once of
my fondness for her. If you do this service to me, I shall assist
you and give you much more than what you expect from me,
or else as you sow, so shall you reap." When I looked at the
paper I saw such a beautiful portrait that I nearly fainted. I
managed myself with great difficulty and said, "Very well, sir.
With Your Majesty's permission I take my leave. God willing
I shall accomplish the task entrusted to me by Your Majesty."

'With these words I took Mubarak with me and left. I
wandered about from place to place in every country and
inquired of every one I happened to meet about the lady whose
portrait I carried with me. Nobody knew anything about her.

No one had even heard of her. For seven years I wandered about facing difficulties and suffering pain till I reached a city. It had magnificent buildings and was densely populated. Everyone there recited the Great Name of God and worshipped Him. I saw there a blind beggar from India begging alms. But no one gave him even a penny or a mouthful of food. I was painfully surprised and took pity on him. Taking out a gold sovereign from my pocket I placed it in his hand. He took it and said, "You are so generous. May God reward you for it. You seem to be a traveller here, not one of this place." I said, "Of course, only today have I arrived in this city. For seven years I have wandered about and ruined myself. But still I have not seen any trace of what I had set out for." The old man blessed me and asked me to follow him. When we reached outside the city I saw a grand mansion. He entered it. I followed him and found that at many places the walls were in disrepair and had given way. I said to myself, "This place could well have been the palace of kings and princes. What a grand palace it must have been indeed when new and in order. Alas, how desolate and deserted does it look now! I don't understand why it is left in this condition. And why does this blind man put up here?" As the blind man went ahead of us, feeling his way with his stick, I heard a voice saying, "Father, I hope all is well. Why have you come back so early today?" The old man said, "Daughter, God made this traveller kind to me. He gave me a gold coin. It is long since I have had a bellyful of good food. I have brought meat and condiments and flour and salt with me. I have also brought some cloth for you. Make yourself clothes from it and wear them. Prepare the food frist so that we may pray for the welfare of this generous man after having our meals. We do not know what he has in his heart but God knows and sees all. May God grant our prayers!"

'When I heard about their starving condition I thought of giving them twenty gold sovereigns more but when I looked towards the place from where the voice had come, I saw a woman who looked exactly like the original of the portrait I had. Comparing it I found there was really no difference at all between the two. A deep sigh issued from my heart and I fainted. Mubarak took me in his arms and began to fan me.

When I recovered I still stared at her. Mubarak asked me, "What is the matter?" I was not yet able to reply when the beautiful lady said, "Fear God, young man. Do not stare at a woman not related to you. Everyone should observe modesty." So nicely did she say these words that I was as struck by her good manners as by her beauty. Mubarak comforted me much but how could he know what I felt in my heart?" Finding myself desperate I said, "O creatures of God, who put up at this place, I am a poor traveller here. It will be so charitable of you if you call me near you and give me a little room to stay." The blind man called me near him and recognizing me by my voice embraced me and conducted me to the quarter where that beautiful woman was. She hid herself in a corner. The old man asked me to relate to him my story, why I had left my home and wandered about and who was it that I had been in search of. I did not mention Malik Sadiq at all and related to him a half-true story saying, "This unfortunate being is the prince of China. My father is still the king. This portrait was purchased from a merchant for many hundred thousand silver coins. Ever since I first saw it I have lost my peace of mind and disguising myself as a mendicant I have wandered about the whole world in search of her and have at last found her here." The old man heaved a sigh and said, "My dear friend, my daughter has been under a curse. No man dare marry and enjoy her love." I said, "Will you please explain it to me?" The old man said:

"'Listen! I was a noble at the king's court, an honourable man of this wretched city. My ancestors were much esteemed and came of a renowned stock. God blessed me with this daughter. When she came of age her beauty and good manners became the talk of the city. They said she was such a beauty that even a fairy or *houri*, far less a human being, would be put to shame before her. The prince of this city also heard all that praise about her beauty and even without seeing her fell in love with her. He gave up taking his meals and confined himself to his own apartment. The king came to know of it and called me in private at night. He proposed marriage between the prince and my daughter. He persuaded me much and finally I accepted. I actually thought that as a daughter had been born to me and had to be married to someone, what could be better than to give her in marriage to a prince? Moreover, the king also would be obliged. Having given him my consent I took my leave. From that very day marriage preparations were made by both the parties. The Qazis and Muftis, the learned and the nobles assembled on an auspicious day and the marriage rites were performed. The bride was taken away in a grand stately manner and all the ceremonies came to a happy end. At night when the bridegroom wished to consummate the marriage, a thundering noise was heard from inside the room. All the guards at the gate were surprised. They attempted to open the door to find out what the matter was. But it was locked securely from the inside and they could not open it. After a short while the noise died down. They broke the door open and found the bridegroom with his head severed and body weltered in blood on the floor. The bride also rolled senseless in her husband's blood and foamed at her mouth. All those present there were shocked by the horrible sight. Such a tragic grief followed those festivities. The news was conveyed to the king. He ran to the spot beating his breast. All the officers of state hurriedly assembled but nobody could unravel the mystery. In his agony the king ordered that the head of the abominable bride too be severed from her body. The moment the king gave this order the thundering noise was heard again. The king was alarmed and ran for his life and ordered the bride to be turned out of the palace. The female attendants brought her to my house. The mysterious event was talked about all over the country and everyone was surprised to hear it. The king and all the citizens here became my enemies because of the prince's murder.

'"When the customary forty days of mourning were over, the king conferred with the officers of state regarding their next step. All of them said, 'Nothing else can be done except that for Your Majesty's consolation and peace of mind the girl, along with her father may be put to death and their property be confiscated.' This punishment was announced and the police chief of the city was ordered to carry it out. He got my house surrounded by guards and blew the trumpet at the gate. But as they made to enter the house to carry out the commands of the king, there was a heavy shower of bricks and stones over them. They could not stand it and ran away wherever they could to save themselves. The king himself heard a dreadful voice in his palace which said, 'Why do you seek your doom? Are you possessed by some demon? If you wish yourself safe and secure, don't be intent on harassing that beauty, or else you will meet the same fate as your son did by marrying her. If you persecute them, you will have to bear terrible consequences too.' The king was so terrified that he fell sick. Immediately he ordered that no one should torture us or have any relations with us and let us remain in our house without oppression.

'"From that very day, the conjurers and exorcists, taking it to be the work of some evil spirit, recite incantations and perform their exorcism to destroy its effects and all the citizens here recite the Qur'an and the Great Name of God. This has been going on, yet the mystery has remained unsolved. I also do not know anything about it. Only once I asked my daughter what she had seen. She said, 'I know nothing except that when my husband wished to perform the nuptial rites, I saw the roof instantly cracked and a throne studded with precious stones appeared through it. A handsome young man in a royal dress was seated on it. There were many persons in his attendance and they prepared themselves to murder the prince. The young man, their chief, came to me and said, "Now, my love, where shall you escape from me?" They had the appearance of men but their feet were like those of goats. My heart palpitated fast and I fainted from fear and anguish. I do not know what happened after that.'

'"Since then the two of us have been living here in this condition. Our friends and relations too have turned their backs on us so as not to offend the king. When I go out to beg alms no one gives me the smallest coin. They do not even like me to stand before their shops. This unfortunate girl has not even a rag to cover her body nor sufficient food to sustain herself. I only wish to God that our lives end soon or that the earth opens and swallows this unfortuante girl. Death is better than a meaningless life like this. God has perhaps sent you for our good that you took pity on me and gave me a coin of gold. We now have good food and clothes for her. We thank God and pray for your welfare. Had she not been possessed by some evil spirit or a jinnee or whatever it is, I would have given her to you as a slave to serve you and would have thought myself fortunate. This is the story of this humble being. Do not think of her and shake off this idea from your mind."

'After hearing this sad story, I earnestly requested the old man to accept me as his son-in-law and said, "Whatever evil my fate has in store for me, let it come." But he did not agree. When the evening set in I came to the serai after taking leave of him. Mubarak said, "Rejoice now, my dear prince. God has made the conditions favourable to you; your labour has not gone to waste." I said, "However much I flattered the blind old man today he did not agree. God knows if he ever will." In such a state of mind I knew no rest for the whole night and wished the day to dawn so that I might go there again. Sometimes I thought that if he should be kind enough to agree, Mubarak would take her to Malik Sadiq. And then I would say to myself, "Well, first let me get her just once, I will somehow persuade Mubarak to let me enjoy her charms." But then I became alarmed at the thought that even if Mubarak agreed, I would meet the same fate as the prince had met at the hands of the djinn, and that how could the king of that country tolerate someone else enjoying her charms while his son had been murdered. In short, the whole night I could not sleep and remained entangled in such disturbing thoughts.

'When it was daylight, I bought some pieces of fine cloth and lace and some fresh and dry fruits from the market and went to the old man. He was pleased to receive me and said, "Life is dearest to all. I will not withhold even my life if it could be of any use to you. I may give my daughter to you just now but I fear that it will put your life in danger and I will have to bear the stigma till the Day of Judgment." I said, "I have no one to help me in this city and you are like a father to me. Consider what pains and troubles I have taken and how I have ruined myself in search of her till I reached here and found her. By the grace of God you have also been kind to me and have consented to give her in marriage to me. But now you are wavering on account of my safety. Please try to be just and think what religion will allow saving one's head from the sword of love and the skull from its dangers. Come what may, I have given myself away in every way. To me life is just the union with my beloved. I may remain alive or I may die, I do not care for it at all. Know it, please, if I remain despairing I will die before my death and you will be responsible for it on the Day of Judgment." In short, one month passed in hope and despair. Everyday I went to the old man and tried to make him agree to my proposal of marriage with his daughter.

'It so happened that the old man fell ill. I devotedly nursed him during his illness. I would carry his urine for check-up to the physician and whatever medicines he prescribed, I administered to the old man as advised. I would also prepare the special food for him and feed him myself. One day he was unusually kind to me and said, "Young man, you are a stubborn fellow. I have told you of all my apprehensions to shake off this idea from your mind. However much I impress upon you that life is most precious and that nothing has any meaning without it, yet you become unnecessarily adamant and determined to jump into the abyss. Well, if you so persist I shall speak of it to my daughter today. Let me see what she says."

. 'O holy men of God, I was overjoyed to hear this good news. I paid my respects to the old man and said, "This is it. Only now have you thought of giving me my life." Taking leave of him I came to my place and passed the whole night talking about it to Mubarak. I even forgot to eat and sleep. Early in the morning I went again to the old man and paid my respects to him. He said, "Well, now I give you my daughter. God bless you. May God protect you both. As long as I live, remain with me. When I am no more you will be free to do as you please."

'A few days later, the old man passed away. We mourned his death and buried his dead body there. After performing the rites on the third day of his death, Mubarak brought the old man's beautiful daughter in a palanquin to the caravanserai and said to me, "As she is, she belongs pure and untouched to Malik Sadiq. Beware, let there be no breach of trust and let not your labours go to waste." I said, "Where is Malik Sadiq here? My heart does not submit. How shall I restrain myself? Come what may, whether I live or die, let me enjoy her charms now." Mubarak lost his patience at this. He threatened me and said, "Don't be childish. In a moment you will find all of it dreadfully changed. Do you think Malik Sadiq cannot reach us here that you want to disobey him? He told you the pros and cons of the matter and warned you of the consequences if you tried to deceive him. If you carry out his commands and take her safe to him he may favourably consider the troubles you have taken for him and may even give her to you because, after all, he is himself a king. And what a great thing it would be: you will continue to be friends with him and get your beloved as well."

'Due to these apprehensions and Mubarak's admonitions I remained disturbed but said nothing. We bought two fast camels and set out for the country of Malik Sadiq. As we went on we heard loud noises coming from a plain. Mubarak said, "Thank God, our fret and toil has not been in vain. Look there, the army of the djinn has arrived." He greeted the djinn and asked them where they were going. They replied, "The king has sent us to receive you. Now we are at your disposal. If you wish, we may carry you there before him in a trice." Mubarak said, "Consider the labour and pain we have taken and that is how God has exalted us in the eyes of the king. Why make haste now? If, God forbid, there is some trouble, our whole labour will go to waste and the king may also be displeased." All of them said, "This is entirely up to you. Proceed as you please." So we journeyed along night and day.

'When we were near the place where the king of the dijnn was and I saw that Mubarak had fallen asleep, I seized the opportunity and fell at that beauty's feet. I burst into tears and earnestly related to her my restlessness and helpless condition because of the threats of Malik Sadiq and said, "Ever since I have seen your portrait I have denied myself food and rest. And now that God has given me this opportunity, I am likely to be separated from you." She said, "I also wish to be with you. Indeed, you have undergone so much trouble and pain for me. I know what you have endured for me. But always remember God and forget me not. Let us see what happens and what the unknown has in store for us." With these words she wept so bitterly that she choked. Such was her condition and so, too, was mine. Mubarak woke up. Seeing us weeping so bitterly he said, "Be comforted, I have an oily lotion with me. I shall rub it on her rose-like body. Its smell will be repulsive to Malik Sadiq and so he may give her to you." We were comforted to hear this. I fondly embraced him and said, "You are like a father to me. My very life was saved because of you. Now also do something that may revive my hopes or else I will die of this grief." He comforted me again.

'When the day dawned, we heard the voices of the djinn and found that many personal attendants of Malik Sadiq had arrived. They had brought two rich robes of honour for us and also a palanquin covered with pearls. Mubarak applied the oil on that beauty's body and got her richly dressed. Then we carried her in the palanquin to Malik Sadiq. The king showed me much respect and exalted me by giving me a seat near him and said, "I shall treat you so nicely as no one has done before. You already have the kingdom of your father for you. Besides, you are now as a son to me." He was talking to me kindly when that fair beauty came before him. The smell of the oil disturbed him. He actually felt so disgusted that, unable to bear it, he went out. He called Mubarak and me after him. Turning to Mubarak he said, "So, this is how you have kept your word! I had warned you that if you deceived me you would fall under my wrath. What smell is this? Now you will see what you receive in return from me!" He was highly offended. Mubarak was so terrified that he loosened his trousers and showing his state of castration said, "Your Majesty, I had set out on this job only after I had got my sign amputated and after applying Solomon-ointment had left it sealed in a box with Your Majesty's Treasurer." Hearing Mubarak's reply, he looked at me indignantly and said, "So it is you who has done it!" He was much enraged and began to rebuke me. It appeared from his looks and whatever he said that he would put me to death. Realizing this, I feared for my life and taking the dagger from Mubarak's girdle, thrust it into the king's belly. He doubled up and staggered. I wondered if I had really killed him for I did not think that the wound was so severe as to cause his death. How was it, then? I was looking at him when he rolled on the ground and turning himself into a ball he soared up into the sky. So high up did he go that he disappeared from sight. After a while like lightning he came down babbling in anger, loud as thunder, and gave me such a kick that I felt dizzy and fell flat on my back and my heart sank. I cannot say how long I lay unconscious. When I recovered I found myself lying in a wilderness where there was nothing but thorn bushes and briars and wild plum-trees. I pulled myself together but could not think of what to do or where to go. Frustrated and despaired, I heaved a sigh and just set out. I inquired of everyone I came across about Malik Sadiq. But everyone took me to be a mad man and said that they had never heard of him.

'One day I climbed a mountain peak and determined to end my life by throwing myself off it. I was about to jump when a veiled rider with his sword, *zul-faqār*, appeared there and said, "Why are you throwing away your life? Man has to suffer pain and misery; your unhappy days are over and the happy ones are ahead. Go to Turkey. Three grief-stricken persons like you have already gone there. Meet them and see the king of that country. The wishes of all five of you will be fulfilled there."

'This is the story of my life. I have presented myself here before you dervishes on the advice of my guide and master, the rescuer of all. I have also the honour of presenting myself before the king and I hope that all of us will be comforted now.'

Denouement

As Azad Bakht and the four dervishes were talking a eunuch came running from the royal seraglio. Bowing low in respect to the king he wished him joy and said, 'Your Majesty, just now a prince has been born. Even the sun and the moon would blush to see his bright face.' The king wondered at the news and said, 'But apparently no one was pregnant there; who has heralded this sun?' The eunuch submitted, 'Mahru, the female attendant of Your Majesty! She has been under Your Majesty's displeasure for some time and has lived forlorn and secluded in the seraglio. No one bothered about her for fear of Your Majesty's wrath. It is she who has given birth to a son bright like the moon by the grace of God.' The king was so overjoyed to hear this that he nearly choked. The four dervishes also blessed him and said, 'May God preserve you! May this son bring you prosperity and grow old under your benign shadow!' The king said, 'This is all due to your gracious presence here for I hadn't even the faintest idea of such a happy event. With your permission I may go and see him.' 'Sure, please do,' they said.

The king went to the seraglio and took the prince in his arms and thanked God. He was happy. He came out and placed the baby at the feet of the dervishes. They blessed him and recited the holy texts to ward off evil influences. The king gave orders to celebrate the occasion. Double trumpets were blown. The royal coffers were opened and the king showed such beneficence and distributed so much money by way of charity that he actually made a pauper a millionaire. All the officers were promoted and their estates doubled. Five years' pay was given as bonus to the troops. The learned and the holy men were granted stipends and lands. The begging bowls and purses of the beggars and destitutes were overfilled with coins of silver and gold. The tillers and farmers were exempted payment of revenue for three years and allowed to keep for themselves whatever they produced. All the people of the city, high and low, rejoiced. They danced with joy and every one of them felt as happy as the king himself.

These festivities and rejoicings were going on when all of a sudden bewailing cries of anguish were heard from inside the seraglio. The private female attendants, the Turkish and the armed women-guards and the eunuchs ran out crying and raising dust over their heads. They said to the king, 'When the prince was given to the nurse after the bath, a cloud descended from the heavens and enveloped them. After a short while the nurse was found lying unconscious on the floor but the baby prince was not there. What a strange calamity has befallen us!' The king was struck dumb to hear the news of these bewildering happenings and the whole country mourned. Nobody cared to take meals for two days; so much did they grieve for the prince. The third day the cloud appeared again. It descended into the seraglio and leaving a cradle studded with precious stones and a covering of pearls, disappeared. The little prince lay in it sucking his thumb. The queen mother immediately took him in her arms and held him to her breast. He wore a fine muslin shirt with a pearl fringe, and his bib was of striped silk. His bracelets and anklets were also studded with precious stones. Toys and bells were placed in the cradle beside him. All the female servants went round him and blessed him saying, 'May ye forever receive your mother's love and live to a good old age!'

The king ordered a grand new palace to be built and after getting it furnished well, hosted the four dervishes there. He himself gave them company whenever he was free from the affairs of his kingdom and personally looked to their comfort. But on the first Thursday of every moon a cloud descended from the heavens and carried the prince away and after two days it brought him back with such presents and toys of different lands that everyone was amazed.

On the seventh birthday of the prince, Azad Bakht, the king, said to the dervishes, 'O men of God, it is not yet known to us who takes away the prince and then brings him back? It is very surprising. Let us see what comes of it.' The dervishes said, 'Do one thing. Put a friendly note in the prince's cradle saying: "Seeing your friendship and kindness I am anxious to meet you. If by way of cordiality you kindly let me know about yourself I shall have my peace of mind, and my wonderment will come to an end." The king wrote a note accordingly on a leaf sprinkled over with gold dust and put it in the golden cradle of the prince.

The prince disappeared as usual. One evening when king Azad Bakht sat conversing with the dervishes, a folded paper fell near him. He opened it and found that it was the reply to his note. It said, 'I am also anxious to see you. A throne is sent herewith. It will be so nice of you to come over here just now. All is arranged here for this festive occasion. It is only you we miss.' The king took the dervishes along with him and sat on the throne.

Like the throne of Solomon, it went up into the air. It rose up and up and then descended at a place where they saw a grand building well-prepared for festivities. But they could not see anyone there. In the meantime someone applied solomon-collyrium on the eyes of all those five men. Two drops of tears fell down from the eyes of each man. They could now see an assembly of beautiful fairies, colourfully attired, to welcome them with a spray of rose-water from containers they held in their hands. As they went further they saw thousands of those beautiful fairies standing respectfully in double rows. In the centre there was an emerald throne and Malik Shahbal, son of Shahrukh, sat on it with majestic airs, reclining on cushions. A lovely girl was playing with Prince Bakhtyar standing by the throne. The nobles were seated on seats arranged in rows on both sides of the throne . Malik Shahbal stood up on seeing Azad Bakht and came down from the throne to embrace him. Taking him by the hand he seated him on the throne beside himself. They talked cordially and the whole day passed in rejoicing and feasting and enjoying dance and music.

The next day Shahbal asked Azad Bakht the reason for

150

bringing the dervishes with him. Azad Bakht related to him all their miseries and woes. He pleaded for them and solicited his help saying, 'They have seen so much misery and pain. It will certainly be kind of you to help them fulfil their wishes. I will be personally grateful to you for this. With your help all their difficulties will be removed.' Malik Shahbal said, 'With all pleasure! You will not find me wanting in carrying out what you say.' With these words, he looked angrily at the fairies and giants around him and wrote to the chiefs of the djinn at different places ordering them to present themselves before him as soon as they received that order, each bringing with him the human being, male or female, he might have in his possession. He also wrote that if anyone of them was late in coming he would be seized and severely punished and that if it was discovered later that anyone of them had concealed any human, he would be crushed in a mill together with his family and no trace of him would remain.

The djinn set out with these orders in all directions. The two kings now sat conversing frankly and cordially. During the talks, Malik Shahbal said to the dervishes, 'I also earnestly wished to have a child and had resolved in my mind that if God gave me a son or a daughter, I would marry it to the offspring of a king of human beings. After I had so resolved in my mind I learnt that the queen was pregnant. With great anxiety I counted each day till at last she had gone the full time and this girl was born. I then ordered all the djinn here to search the four corners of the world and to carefully bring a prince to me of whatever king. The djinn immediately left and after a short while they brought this prince to me. I thanked God and took the child in my arms. Actually I came to love him more than my own daughter, so much so that even for a moment I do not like him to remain away from me. But I send him back considering that his parents will be worried if they do not see him. So I get him here once a month and after keeping him with me for a couple of days, send him back. Now that we have met, I will get them married if God wills it so. We are all mortal beings. Let us see their marriage performed whilst we are alive.' King Azad Bakht was pleased to note the cordiality of Shahbal and to hear of his proposal and said, 'The mystery of the prince's frequent disappearances has been set at rest. Take this son as your own now. Do for him as you please.' The two kings grew more intimate. They had a good time together.

Within ten or twelve days, mighty kings of Iram and from the High Mountains and Islands, who had been called, arrived at Shahbal's court. First of all Malik Sadiq was ordered to produce the human being he had in his possession. He felt baffled and sad but he had to produce the beautiful girl before him. Then the djinn king of Ammān was ordered to present his daughter for whom the prince of Neemroz, the bull rider, had gone mad. He made many excuses but at last had to present her. When the daughter of the king of Farang and Behzad Khan were demanded, all those present there said that they had no knowledge of them. They even swore by Solomon. But when finally the king of the Ocean of Qulzum (Red Sea) was asked, he kept silent and lowered his head. Malik Shahbal treated him kindly and urging him on oath, gave him hopes of elevating him and then threatened him. At last he joined his hands together in submission and said, 'Your Majesty, the truth is that when the king of Persia came to the river to receive his son, and the prince out of eagerness plunged his horse into the waters, I was out hunting and happened to pass that way at that time. I had stopped there to behold the scene. When the mare of the princess also plunged into the waters with her I chanced to look at the princess and was struck by her beauty. I immediately asked the djinn to bring the princess and her mare safe to me. Behzad Khan too plunged his horse after her. When he was also to be drowned, I admired his bravery and gallantry. So I got him picked up too. They are safe and secure with me.' Relating all this, he sent for them and presented them before Shahbal. Then they made a great search for the daughter of the king of Damascus. All those present there were interrogated strictly but with politeness. No one acknowledged or said anything about her. Malik Shahbal then asked if any king or chief was absent. The djinn humbly submitted, 'All have presented themselves except *Musalsal Jadu* who has built a fort by means of magic on the Mountain Qāf at the end of the world. Because of his arrogance he has not presented himself. We, Your Majesty, are not able to bring him here by force. It is a difficult rocky place and he himself is a big devil.'

Malik Shahbal was full of anger to hear this. He sent forth an army of winged and skilful djinn with the orders: 'Better if he comes with the princess of his own accord; otherwise bring him here with his hands tied behind his neck, raze his fort to the ground and destroy his country.' Immediately a large army marched towards that place and in a day or two brought that haughty and rebellious chief in chains before Malik Shahbal. He asked him again and again about the princess but that haughty fellow would not confess. At last Malik Sahabal was filled with rage and ordered, 'Cut this wretched one to pieces and fill his skin with chaff.' He also ordered the winged ones to go to Mountain Qāf and search for the princess. They went there and finding her brought her to Malik Shahbal. All those prisoners and the four dervishes were pleased to see the justness and charity of Malik Shahbal and invoked the blessings of God on him. They all rejoiced. King Azad Bakht too was much pleased. Malik Shahbal then asked the men to be conducted to the Hall of Private Audience and the women to the royal seraglio. He ordered the city to be richly decorated and illuminated. He also ordered to make preparations for the marriage. All this was done in no time, as if they had been already expecting these orders. A happy hour was fixed and he got Prince Bakhtyar married to his daughter Roshan Akhtar. The young merchant of Yemen (the first dervish) was married to the princess of Damascus; the prince of Persia (the second dervish) to the princess of Basra; the prince of Ajam (the third dervish) to the princess of Farang. The daughter of the king of Neemroz was given in marriage to Behzad Khan and the daughter of the djinn king of Ammān was given in marriage to the prince of Neemroz. The prince of China (the fourth dervish) was married to the daughter of the old man of Ajam, who had been in the prison of Malik Sadiq. Thus, with the assistance of Malik Shahbal each of those unhappy persons got what he wanted. The celebrations continued for forty days and they all rejoiced night and day.

At the end of the celebrations Malik Shahbal gave each prince rich presents and rarities and they all set out for their respective countries fully satisfied and safely reached there and began to reign. Behzad Khan and the young merchant of Yemen chose to remain with king Azad Bakht of their own accord. The merchant was made the Chief Steward and Behzad Khan the Army Chief of the fortunate prince Bakhtyar. So long as they lived, they lived in prosperity.

Just as God fulfilled the wishes of king Azad Bakht and the four dervishes, may He through His beneficence and kindness, and by the Five Pure Bodies, the twelve Imams and by the Fourteen Innocents (God bless them all), also grant the wishes of all those who are in despair. Amen!

Epilogue

When this book was completed by the grace of God, I thought of writing a chronogram which may give its year as well. I started writing it in AH 1215 (AD 1801). For want of time I could finish it only in early AH 1217 (1803). As I reflected, the name *Bāgh-o-Bahār* seemed to be most appropriate as it also gave the year when it was completed*. So I gave it this name. Reading it will be like taking a walk in a garden in full bloom. But while a garden is always exposed to autumn, this work is not. It will remain green, as ever:

> *When this book was completed*
> *The year was A.H. 1217*
> *Keep it before you night and day;*
> *From Bāgh-o-Bahār, its name,*
> *You may know its year of completion..*
> *Vagaries of autumn it does not know;*
> *It is spring, the vernal season, fresh, as ever.*
> *I have nourished it with my heart's blood;*
> *Pieces of my heart are its fruits and leaves.*

---

* Letters of the Urdu alphabet have been given numerical values which are mainly used to compose a chronogram. The practice is to form a brief sentence or phrase, the numerical values of all the letters in which add up to give the year, mostly according to the Hijri era, when the event took place. The Hijri era begins from AD 622—the year of the Prophet's migration from Mecca. Thus, the numerical value of the letters used in *Bāgh-o-Bahār* add up to AH 1217, which corresponds to AD 1802-3 of the Christian era.

All will forget me when I pass away;
As a souvenir this, my book, will live.
Whoever reads it may please remember me;
To him I do say:
If there be any error, ignore it, please,
For where there is a rose, there is a thorn.
Man is prone to err;
Howsoever careful he is, he will fail;
I wish no more than what I pray:
O God, may I always remember Thee!
Only thus may I pass my time night and day;
may I not be harshly taken
To account for my deeds
In the night of the grave
And on Judgment Day!
O God, for the sake of Thy Prophet
Shower Thy favours on me
In this world and in the next!

Selected Glossary

Abu Jahal an enemy of Muhammad, Prophet of Islam

Ahmad Shah a Mughal emperor deposed and blinded in 1754

Ahmad Shah Abdali/Durrani an Afghan ruler who led several expeditions into India between 1748-67

Ali the son-in-law of Prophet Muhammad, and the fourth Caliph

Amir Khusrau a great Persian poet of India (d.1325)

Āzar name of Abraham's father, an idol-maker

Baiju Bawra a celebrated Indian musician of 16th century

Farang a generic term to include almost all the European countries

Farhad the 'Mountain-digger', a celebrated Persian lover of *Shirin*

Fasli an era instituted by the Mughal emperor Akbar (r.1556-1605)

Five Pure Bodies Muhammad the Prophet, his daughter Fatimah, his son-in-law Ali, his grandsons Husan and Husain

Fourteen Innocents Prophet Muhammad, his daughter Fatimah, and *the twelve Imams*

Ghilman boys who attend the virtuous in paradise

Gusā'īn a Hindu fakir

Hatim name of a generous tribal chief of Arabia

Ibrahim ibn Adham the prince of Balkh (Bactria) who gave up the throne for the happiness of perfect poverty

Iram the fabulous gardens said to have been devised in emulation of the gardens of paradise

Kabir a renowned saint-poet of 15th century India whose

157

imagery combines Muslim and Hindu ideas

Khizr the mystical guide, the prophet-saint who discovered and drank of the water of life, whereby he became immortal. He is believed to help those who are in distress or have lost their way

Kisra name given to Naushervan the Just (531-578), or any of the kings of Persia

Laila the dark-complexioned beloved of *Majnun* of Arabia

Lāt an idol worshipped by the pagan Arabians

Manāt an idol worshipped by the pagan Arabians

Nizamuddin Auliya a great Muslim saint of India (d.1325)

Padmini a woman of the first and most excellent of the four classes into which the sex is divided

Qāf the world-embracing mountain range; the abode of the djinn and fairies;

Rustam a legendary warrior of Persia

Shab-e-Barat the night in mid-*Sha'ban*, the eighth month of the lunar calendar, during which sins are forgiven and destinies fixed; a vigil is observed with prayers, feasting, illuminations and fireworks

Shab-e-Qadr the mystic Night of Power (or Honour), in which Revelation comes down to a benighted world and transforms all conflicts into peace and harmony

Shivrat/Shivratri Shiva's night, a Hindu festival in honour of Shiva

Suraj Mal Jat a warrior statesman who extended Bharatpur kingdom

Tansen a celebrated Indian musician of 16th century

Urdū lit. a camp

Urdū-e-Mu'allā lit. an exalted camp

Yusuf Joseph, a prophet whose brothers flung him into a well out of jealousy

Zu'l-faqār name of 'Ali's sword

THE STORY OF PENGUIN CLASSICS

Before 1946 ...'Classics' are mainly the domain of academics and students, without readable editions for everyone else. This all changes when a little-known classicist, E. V. Rieu, presents Penguin founder Allen Lane with the translation of Homer's *Odyssey* that he has been working on and reading to his wife Nelly in his spare time.

1946 *The Odyssey* becomes the first Penguin Classic published, and promptly sells three million copies. Suddenly, classic books are no longer for the privileged few.

1950s Rieu, now series editor, turns to professional writers for the best modern, readable translations, including Dorothy L. Sayers's *Inferno* and Robert Graves's *The Twelve Caesars*, which revives the salacious original.

1960s The Classics are given the distinctive black jackets that have remained a constant throughout the series's various looks. Rieu retires in 1964, hailing the Penguin Classics list as 'the greatest educative force of the 20th century'.

1970s A new generation of translators arrives to swell the Penguin Classics ranks, and the list grows to encompass more philosophy, religion, science, history and politics.

1980s The Penguin American Library joins the Classics stable, with titles such as *The Last of the Mohicans* safeguarded. Penguin Classics now offers the most comprehensive library of world literature available.

1990s The launch of Penguin Audiobooks brings the classics to a listening audience for the first time, and in 1999 the launch of the Penguin Classics website takes them online to a larger global readership than ever before.

The 21st Century Penguin Classics are rejacketed for the first time in nearly twenty years. This world famous series now consists of more than 1300 titles, making the widest range of the best books ever written available to millions – and constantly redefining the meaning of what makes a 'classic'.

The Odyssey continues ...

The best books ever written

PENGUIN CLASSICS

SINCE 1946

Find out more at www.penguinclassics.com